T0208478

THE
FALSE PROPHETS
AND THE GOOD
CATHOLIC PRIEST

THE
FALSE PROPHETS
AND THE GOOD
CATHOLIC PRIEST

STEVEN KWAME MENDS

THE FALSE PROPHETS AND THE GOOD CATHOLIC PRIEST

Scripture quotations marked KJV are from the Holy Bible, King James Version (Authorized Version). First published in 1611. Quoted from the KJV Classic Reference Bible, Copyright © 1983 by The Zondervan Corporation.

Scripture quotations marked NIV are taken from the Holy Bible, New International Version®. NIV®. Copyright © 1973, 1978, 1984 by International Bible Society. Used by permission of Zondervan. All rights reserved. [Biblica]

iUniverse books may be ordered through booksellers or by contacting:

iUniverse
1663 Liberty Drive
Bloomington, IN 47403
www.iuniverse.com
1-800-Authors (1-800-288-4677)

Because of the dynamic nature of the Internet, any web addresses or links contained in this book may have changed since publication and may no longer be valid. The views expressed in this work are solely those of the author and do not necessarily reflect the views of the publisher, and the publisher hereby disclaims any responsibility for them.

Any people depicted in stock imagery provided by Getty Images are models, and such images are being used for illustrative purposes only. Certain stock imagery © Getty Images.

ISBN: 978-1-6632-0011-2 (sc)
ISBN: 978-1-6632-0012-9 (e)

Print information available on the last page.

iUniverse rev. date: 05/23/2020

CHAPTER 1

It was a Monday morning. It seemed the sun had come up earlier than usual filling the sky with abundant rays of light in spite of the cottony cumulus clouds which occupied most parts of the, otherwise, fine blue sky. It had a slight chill in it. Araba stood in front of her compound wearing an old blue sweater, which had two buttons missing.

She had a newly bought broom in her right hand but instead of going on with the routing sweeping of the morning, she was rather deep in thought and pondering on her past. She remembered she married her husband before she even had her first menses. It wasn't uncommon then, for, she had been betrothed to him before she was born. She was thus, as the people called it, an asiwa.

Her husband had been her sole financial supporter from the day she was born so she owed him a great debt and even though she had not liked him, she had borne his twelve children without complaint. She was still young and actually enjoyed her circumstances with all the children because, as she claimed, the best children always come later in life. Her fecundity was also marked by mortality since she and her husband had buried four children at the cemetery at Tafo in Kumasi.

Kumasi was the epitome of cities in Ghana. Compared to other cities and towns in the country, it was sprawling with suburbs like Adum Ashanti New Town, Fante New Town, Asafo, Bantama and Amakom. By early independence, it had achieved the enviable status of the Garden City of West Africa. The Ashantis were and are still proud of the city. Most of its houses are communal with several different families living in the same compound. Araba and her husband chose to settle outside one of these compounds in a two-room tenement at a once-lonely suburb of Amakom. With her eight children and a husband, she had moved from the once-dignified town of Anomabo, thanks to the early white settlers, to come and seek greener pastures among the brave Ashantis of Kumasi.

They were well received, yet Araba would not entertain friendships with anyone as she maintained that friends were always busybodies and that her own business must be hers alone. With regard to friends, therefore, she was fiercely independent.

Their location at Amakom suited them well. There was an elementary school a stone-throw to the north of their house. The market place, always bustling with intense activity, was about three hundred meters north east of the house. The communal tap, hardly kept clean, was west of the house while the Catholic Church, of which Araba and her husband were originally members, was also in close quarters in a rather solitary south end.

Almost every year or two, the family managed to send once child to school. However, just as the last child entered class one, a strange illness afflicted the husband and he was about to give up the ghost. His subsequent unexpected death was too abrupt and chaotic for her and the rest of the family and it certainly posed a big and novel problem for her. She should have anticipated the death because before that, she said she had seen and heard an owl on their roof some days back, and to her, it was a really bad omen to see the bird let alone hear it hoot too.

"Mama, what are we going to do? I think I will quit school and get a job to help in the family's upkeep," Kwesi, the brilliant elder son, said to the mother.

Araba, and illiterate, and a woman of foresight, and also aware of her child's shining academic record told Kwesi,

"No, you can't quit school. I will surely see you all through for you to know that despite the uphill task I am also a capable woman even without a husband."

"Are you sure you can handle it?" Kwesi was still apprehensive.

"Why are you so doubtful? You must have faith in your mother. Have I been a bad mother thus far?"

"No, mama."

"Then stay your apprehension."

Though relatively young at the death of her husband, she thought she would never marry again. The colossal burden of raising the children single-handed was a challenge to her womanhood. Her days began at dawn when she assiduously prepared food items to sell in the market. Her baked bread was a very sellable delicacy at the marketplace and this eased her anguish a great deal. At the crack of dawn, fire would be in the oven and by six thirty, hot loaves of bread would be ready for Kwesi, Kojo, and Esi to sell. The hot loaves sold readily in the active market place around seven to seven thirty when many villagers brought their wares to it. In the meantime, Araba saw to the bathing of her younger children and feeding them to prepare for school. The older bread vendors joined them after having sold the bread and having eaten their breakfast while on the way home.

Just like their mother, the children, especially the older ones, were not indolent. They were industrious both at home and at school. Their academic excellence caught the attention of the head teachers who, every now and then, called Araba to school and notified her of the very good performance of her children.

"They are all doing well rest assured." The head teacher's attitude was just out of compassion for her.

"I think Kwesi and Kojo must go on to secondary school. I am sure they'll come out with flying colors at the entrance examination," she said.

Such gracious comments boosted Araba's morale a great deal. She continued with the bread baking and she also went to the market place to sell fish. On account of her assiduity, she was able to feed, clothe, and shelter the children with a little above average nourishment and clothing. None of the children was ever seriously sick except for a touch of fever here and there which even diminished in the shortest possible time.

When it came to the time for Kwesi and Kojo to take their entrance examination to secondary school, Araba did not hesitate to pay their registration fees. As if foreordained, it rained cats and dogs on the very day the children were to take the examination. They were supposed to walk to T.I Ahmadiyya Secondary School. As Araba didn't have raincoats or umbrellas for her children, they were forced to use their mother's cover cloth over their heads. Nonetheless, they were still drenched on their arrival at the school. They had no towels or anything so they took off their soaked shirts and singlets and sat bare-chested to write the examination. They shivered and their teeth chattered as they took the examination. Regardless of the natural obstacle, they were not spared by an easy examination. They admitted it was the hardest in their young lives yet, and in a matter of about two and a half months, Kwesi and Kojo came home from school beaming ear-to-ear smiles. They had passed with merit and were able to obtain scholarships and bursaries. Araba's ecstasy was profound. She, painstakingly, bought items for her children and admonished them saying,

"You know our situation and since a good opportunity has come our way, it's up to you to do your best."

Kwesi, as if to relieve his mother's apprehension said,

"Mama, as long as the good Lord gives us life and health, I, for one, will not disappoint you. I will study very hard and I plan to take my education far."

"I, too, will not squander this opportunity to prove to you and myself that I can do it." Kojo also said, his eyes blurred with emotional tears.

According to Araba, in order to guard against the activities of witches and their witchcraft on her two sons, she, for some reason known to her alone, summarily, left the Catholic Church to join one of the mushrooming spiritual churches. Her superstitious beliefs became evident after she joined the church. She had cause to have faith in the church because, somehow, whether it was coincidence or otherwise, one neighbor's daughter had been healed of epilepsy by the church's prophetess. From then onwards, whatever the prophets said was the immaculate truth.

The spiritual church was built with corrugated iron sheets, which made the sweltering heat from the midday sun rather intolerable. It had a concrete floor, which was good because all the members of the congregation had to remove their shoes and sandals before entering the church. To the left of the church stood the big, white, wooden cross under which special prayers were said. There was a well with whose water, holy water as claimed by the prophetess, the congregation used to bathe, drink and sprinkle in their rooms to avert evil spirits. Members of the congregation were resourceful, as they had cultivated a farm and a fishpond for the prophetess. Under the thatched roof was the small but hopeful kindergarten and elementary school.

During church service, the place was like a disco. The very many women were there to enjoy themselves with all kinds of dances, whether secular or sacred. The drums thumped away, the trumpet blasted and the maracas jingled, intermittently punctuated by loud bellows of,

"Praise the Lord."

"Alleluia."

"Praise him, the Lord"

"Paradise."

"We shall be there"

"Paradise"

"We are all there"

No wonder the church was full of women. The holy water was the symbol of the church service. Sprinkling of it, maybe copied from the Catholic Asperges, started and ended the service. The collection was the highlight of the service for, every member of the congregation had to get up from his or her seat, it was a must to do so, and dance right up to the collection barrel placed conspicuously in front of the prophetess, and she watched the barrel with an eagle's eye not to miss anything. Members were asked to come to the barrel as often as they could because God wanted a cheerful giver and the more you gave the more favors you received from the Almighty. Church service could last anywhere between five to six hours. During this time, members claimed they were possessed with the apparent spirit of glossolalia or speaking in tongues. There were too many of them and the prayer session was one noisy clatter. It was so spontaneous that it seemed incredulous to the unfamiliar ear.

After Kwesi and Kojo had had a very successful first term, they came home to face the persuasions of Araba to join the spiritual church and be baptized. They had already been baptized in the Catholic Church when their father was alive. She claimed that that way, they would be protected spiritually and from every tenet of witchcraft and the devil. Certainly, according to Araba, it was common knowledge that a spiritual church did wonders in that aspect.

Kwesi noted that his mother's insistence would permanently make all her children members of the church. He detested the idea and showed marked resistance to his mother's pleas. He said,

"Dada was a staunch Catholic and I want to remain so. Moreover, my school and Kojo's are Catholic schools and, to me, there is nothing wrong with their teachings despite the many accusations of the not-so-sure churches of their own survival and evangelism. Mama, how do you expect me to divert my Catholic spirituality to a rather young church like this one?"

"You are a child. I still want you to join."

"Where would this church be in ten years?" Kwesi asked Araba, with evident resentment,

"Catholic priests never have time for the masses who throng the church but in a spiritual church the congregation is fewer and you receive much individual attention from the prophets and the prophetesses," she said.

"Mama beware of these people you call prophets and prophetesses; they could be false ones you know."

"You are such a child indeed. I am older and your mother as well. Don't ever forget that I know better and what is good for you."

Araba let things go their natural course with Kwesi. She had no other choice but she was undoubtedly aggrieved to see her son go his own way without any kind of spiritual protection as she called it.

Koio had, thus, easily become the favorite child of his mother. He conceded that his mother's native intelligence was too fragile for academic intrusion and therefore there was no argument from him.

He always sprinkled himself and his surroundings with the holy water prescribed by the prophetess. He never forgot to burn the incense also given him by the prophetess, once again, to cast away the omnipresent evil spirits and demons. Before long, he submerged himself totally in the spiritual church. This pleased his mother and the prophetess immensely.

"You know the prophetess was a Catholic herself but when she wasn't satisfied with the church's teachings and when, according to her, the Holy Spirit descended upon her she went and founded her own church which, as you see today, is bustling with much life," Araba confided in her son, Kojo.

"That's the reason why there are some striking resemblances to the Catholic service," Kojo said.

"Never mind Kwesi's insolence. When the witches and other evil spirits get the better of him, he'll run here very fast."

CHAPTER 2

During the fourth year of school, Kwesi and Kojo had both grown taller. Kwesi was a hair taller than Kojo but Kojo had slowly taken on the good looks of their mother. Kwesi's strength seemed phenomenal, and no wonder, he threw the shotput, discuss and the javelin for his school, He was very good at them and was the current champion in the Central Region. He trained hard.

Lithesome Kojo had the legs of a runner and was, consistently, doing well in the four hundred meters. If only Kojo would train harder he could be a champion like his brother. He always thought training was for women and depended solely on his natural talent much unlike Kwesi. Their fellow students and friends liked them a lot because they were both academically and athletically good. Soon, after the second term of many sporting activities, their schools vacated. They came home and were shocked. Their sister, Esi, also a teenager, was pregnant. It was common knowledge that Kofi was Esi's boyfriend but he denied responsibility for her pregnancy.

Araba consulted the prophetess on Esi's pregnancy and the prophetess agreed that she would do something for Araba and her daughter as the daughter was rather too young to become a mother. She was fourteen.

"What something could be done by this prophetess other than induced abortion," Araba was weighed down by this thought.

"I have prayed for teenagers who didn't want their pregnancies and they had been spared of them." The prophetess said.

"How your holiness?"

"You should have faith in me because prayer does wonders," She bellowed the statement out and at once went into an apparent trance and speaking in tongues to God.

Araba, immediately, believed her much as the prophetess' transfiguration surprised her.

"I will bring Esi, I will bring her," she said as if marveling at the prophetess' power.

D-o-o-o br-ing her, Jesus, d-o-o-o Br-i-ng her, dooo briiing her," the prophetess said this like a fetish priest.

"When should I bring her, your holiness?"

"Now, of course, J-e-esus, J-e-e-e-sus, Je-e-sus."

"Amen," Araba said and asked to go. She hurried home and found Esi deep in thought.

"Come on, put some good clothes on and let's go to the prophetess, bad girl," she said feigning anger and emphasizing the last couple of words.

"Mama, why?" Esi said with a tremulous voice.

"Why? Shut up and don't ask me foolish questions!"

"I don't want to go anywhere because I feel ashamed."

"You feel ashamed?!" Shame on you. Who asked you to be running around, small girl like you?"

She grabbed her by the left ear and tried to pull her up. Esi was already crying.

"You are going for prayers. The prophetess will pray to God to rid you of this stupid pregnancy, shame."

"Leave me alone."

Araba was angry so she gave Esi two quick, hard slaps on the right cheek and pushed her into the bedroom. Her younger children stood and trembled in the corner. Esi, finally, got her blouse and cloth on and they were off to the prophetess.

Upon arrival at the church premises, the prophetess was busy praying and counting some large rosaries. She had noticed Araba and

Esi but kept praying and counting for another ten minutes before finally coming to them.

"Praise the Lord," she said.

"Alleluia," Araba and Esi said in unison while Esi looked down and couldn't look at the prophetess in the face.

"Esi, you are pregnant by two months and with Kofi. You have gone to such and such a place for your wrong doing but I will help you."

Esi, especially, was taken aback because what the prophetess was saying was true.

"How could she know that?" She thought. "She must indeed have power."

"Araba, you can leave her with me tonight. Remember, I will do this free of charge but after I have finished and you are satisfied with my power you can bring your reward you deem fit. Praise the Lord."

"Alleluia, thank you prophetess. I will do my best." Araba said and left.

It happened that it wasn't only a prayer session; it was part of it. The prophetess had some powerful potions which she administered to Esi orally and in an enema. The prophetess had done this to several girls and never said a word about it. This time luck was not on her side because Esi collapsed immediately into an apparent fainting spell.

The prophetess quickly went for water and splashed it on her in an effort to revive her but there was no success. The last resort was to take her to the nearby private hospital. The doctor did his professional best to help but he too failed. He advised the prophetess to take her to Okomfo Anokye Hospital.

"Oh can't you do something?"

"Just pray hard. You are a prophetess. The girl is dying."

"Oh God," the prophetess said and with a lot of butterflies in her stomach she got help and put Esi in a taxi and they were bound for Okomfo Anokye.

Yes there, the doctors pronounced Esi dead on arrival. Upon knowledge of Esi's death, no grief surpassed that of the children. Kwesi was shattered. For some reason incomprehensible to her children, Araba never shifted blame to the prophetess. Not that she didn't expect something fishy, the prophetess was exonerated as grief-stricken Araba still surprisingly maintained that the prophetess was infallible.

Kwesi found enough reason to exhort Kojo to quit the church, as it was obvious that the prophetess was vulnerable to mortal corruption. He outlined to Kojo the constant use of juju, witchcraft, black power and occultism in their day-to-day activities in church. How Kwesi knew all these since he didn't attend church service at the spiritual church baffled Kojo, but he asked,

"Does that mean that Mama is perhaps a witch who collaborates with other witches to seemingly wreak havoc on herself?"

"It could be. Physically, it seems she is tormented but, spiritually, she is not. Just think of the history of our family. Five children and Papa have died. Do you think it's just coincidence? She could be a witch, I tell you!" Kwesi said.

"Don't say that about your own mother. I know our superstitious nature, and, what we can't explain, we attribute to witchcraft. Some of the deaths in the family could be due to some unfortunate hereditary ailment in the family; sickle cell maybe."

Was Araba actually a witch? Kojo loved his mother and could not reconcile such a serious question with reality. He still went to the spiritual church with his mother.

In order to escape his mother's tenacious hold on spirituality, Kwesi sought to partake in the annual essay competition through which teenagers were chosen to travel abroad, especially to America. He was successful and was awarded a year's scholarship to study in a high school in America. Kwesi embraced his new luck and prepared himself physically and psychologically for travel abroad. Surprisingly, Araba did not want her son to go outside the country but her incessant pleas to stop him fell flat.

"Going abroad is an opportunity to advance and such rare luck must not be squandered," Kwesi told his mother firmly.

"You need spiritual protection then. Our church prophetess can do wonders in that respect."

"There you go again with your spiritual leader."

"Kwesi, this blessing could be a misfortune. I insist on your coming to see us in church," Araba said.

Kwesi never paid any attention to his mother and sought help from some relatives and on the 18th July, he was on the plane with thirteen other students despite the inclement weather and without the blessing of his mother and protection from the prophetess. But did he actually need them? Kojo, who had accompanied his brother, said a tearful farewell and was off to Kumasi the same day.

After getting to know his Ghanaian compatriots, Kwesi realized that when it came to status, he was only a midget because the other students were all sons and daughters of men and women of consequence. They were the Ghanaian bourgeois. His inferiority complex gnawed at him but he later mustered enough confidence to communicate with the others.

Suddenly, they were jerked backwards by the forward motion of the plane. The fasten your seat belt sign was lit and a gorgeous hostess of the Pan Am Boeing aircraft stood at the front aisle and gave instructions and directions on how to react in case of an emergency. They flew without any mishaps and after some hours the plane touched down at Dakar airport for refueling.

On resumption of travel, though, as if the witches were following Kwesi, the plane developed engine trouble over the Atlantic. With sheer dedication, a touch of professionalism and some really weird luck the captain and his crew managed to let all passengers get in their life jackets. As if the impending disaster had been foreordained, the aircraft plunged into the Atlantic. Most of the passengers floated effortlessly on the sea. The initial panic had been quelled, nevertheless, the survivors, Kwesi included, were not spared a moment of relief in their frightful situation as it suddenly started to storm. Their ordeal lasted about an hour with the claws of death so very near while many of the passengers had given up hope. Kwesi, full of courage and with his faith asserting itself, prayed steadfastly for divine and providential intervention. His prayers were answered because in the vicinity of the crash a fishing vessel was fast approaching as if the captain of the vessel has been alerted by radio of the accident. Through binoculars, he spotted the languishing former passengers of the plane and set out immediately to their rescue. Despite, the rain, the physical and mental exhaustion, Kwesi and most of the passengers were rescued. A few unlucky passengers were either drowned or lost.

Immediately they were on land again, reporters rushed to them to get a first-hand account of their close call. Their stories made headlines and they were instant celebrities. The captain and the surviving crewmembers were heroes. The instant fame was meaningless to Kwesi who vowed not to travel ahead to the U.S. as planned. He begged the authorities to return him to his country by any means other than by plane. In a few weeks he was bundled to Accra. Here, too, he was surprised at the crash of reporters.

When, finally, Kwesi was in Kumasi with his mother and the rest of the family, he related to them in a piecemeal manner what happened to him.

"The witches were after you" Araba was quick to point out. A sneezing urge came upon her and she let out a very loud sneeze, spattering some saliva and phlegm. After she used the corner of her cover cloth as a handkerchief, she said,

"This sneeze even clearly tells me that what I said about witches was true."

"Maybe, but I think it was just ill luck," Kwesi, in a definite attempt to always contradict his mother said. But Araba insisted and also said,

"Let's go and see our prophetess and see what she says about your very bad ordeal."

At first, Kwesi maintained his doubts but Kojo and the rest of the family went to the spiritual church service. The place jostled with constant drumming, singing, and dancing, clapping, and speaking in tongues. The congregations were hero-worshipping their so-called prophetess. Surprising how she could wield so much intense power.

The highlight of the service was the 'adansedie' or testimony time. At that point, a very tall man danced majestically to the front of the well-attended service and bellowed out,

"Praise the Lord"

"Alleluia"

"God"

"He is a miracle worker"

"Paradise"

"We shall be there"

"Paradise"

"We are there already"

After all these appellations, he began his testimony.

"Last week, the god of our prophetess displayed his magnanimous powers to me in a very grand way. I had traveled with some friends to the border at Aflao. Unfortunately for us, there were clashes between soldiers on both sides of the border. Because of the undesirable state of affairs, my friends and I took a detour and decided to cross the border through a bush path. Here again, there was the same problem of fighting. We were shot at and believe it or not one of my friends, so deeply immersed in native medicine, could just catch the bullets with his bare hands. The man ordered us to lie prostrate on the ground. In the meantime, the man with the black medicine had become invisible. Our most dangerous time came when the soldiers came to make sure we were actually dead. We lay stone-still. We were trampled on. Praise the Lord"

"Alleluia"

"We dared not move and we lay stiff although shivering in our insides in the dirt all that seemingly eternal time. The soldiers finally departed and the friend who had gone invisible returned to his physical form. During that most dangerous time, you know what I was doing?"

"No, what?" the congregation, mostly women exclaimed.

"All that time, I was praying hard to the god of our dear prophetess to intervene and I know definitely well that the name of the prophetess did wonders. I have with me three million cedis, a packet of candles and incense as my present to our prophetess and her wonderful god. Praise the Lord"

"Alleluia."

"This is the end of my testimony."

The prophetess stood up, blessed the man with the sign of the cross and said,

"Your belief in my power and my god saved you. You need to come to my special prayers. Such prayers are categorized. There are prayers for one million cedis, others are for two million and up to ten million cedis. The greater your amount of money, the greater the power of the prayers. Here is a bottle of Florida water and holy water for your spiritual upkeep," she said and wiped her brows with a white handkerchief and assumed a rather pious stance.

The tall man got the bottle and bowed reverently and said thank you. After this the drums went "tam tam" again and many women danced up in front and put money in the collection barrel again and again. After a protracted time of singing and dancing, the prophetess rang the bell to quieten the agitation that had arisen due to the seemingly credible tone of the last speaker's witnessing. Silence descended upon the congregation and another member, this time a woman with a small baby witnessed again.

After the third woman's testimony, Araba urged Kwesi to go in front and attribute his recent ordeal to the saving power of the prophetess. Kwesi disappointed his mother by going out of the church. He waited outside after finding out that his shoes had been stolen.

In spite of Kwesi's unruly behavior, according to Araba, she was delighted that her difficult son had attended service after all with them even though he didn't sit through the service.

"Did you believe the hoax about a man becoming invisible?" Kwesi couldn't wait to ask. He gesticulated to mean he didn't believe it.

"You are just a child; you don't believe anything. We have good and bad medicine that can do virtually miraculous things here. It wasn't even just the medicine alone but also the saving power of the prophetess when he called upon her and her god for assistance."

"What was the significance of the sale of special prayers to the members?"

"She doesn't work other than saving people, you know," she had the pleasure of seeing Kwesi's countenance brighten up. She thought Kwesi was finally coming to his senses but Araba was disappointed by Kwesi's next question. He asked,

"But the money involved in this case is too much. Moreover, there is the constant request for collection. Isn't the collection enough for her."

"You are too full of questions, Kwesi, just have faith as mother said," Kojo who had thoroughly enjoyed himself at the service and claimed he had spoken in tongues finally contributed and smirked delectably.

The church service had not put Kwesi's mind to rest. He brooded about the idea that he had sinned because he had missed the Catholic mass. He was also angry about his stolen shoes. Moreover, he had not been impressed by the prophetess and the whole copy-cat structure of her service. He was not ready to believe a prophetess who was illiterate and yet claimed to know the Bible through and through. One thing that impressed Kwesi though was the prophetess's power of divination. Maybe she had some supernatural powers after all.

What came into Kwesi's mind was to see the Catholic parish priest. He solicited the help of Kojo to accompany him but Kojo declined the invitation on the grounds that he had left the church for good. Kwesi only smiled at what he thought was his mother's or brother's obstinacy and the whole idea of the spiritual church.

Kwesi went alone to the Amakom parish. He wanted to be in the confessional for having sinned. The cook called the attention of the priest and, without delay, he came out in his immaculate white cassock.

"What can I do for you?" His question was followed by a cheerful smile. Kwesi was encouraged and, though, burdened by the guilt, he was forced to smile back. The smile was as infectious as a yawn.

"I want to come to confession," he said coyishly.

"Very good but just a second." He went inside and got a blue rosary and a book of prayers. When he returned to the confessional, Kwesi had crouched in one of the front pews. The priest waited patiently, also immersed in contemplative meditation. Kwesi said the Lord's Prayer over four times and also the "Hail Mary" three times. Finally, he crossed himself and knelt before the priest who was partially concealed by the gauzy curtain at the confessional.

"Bless me father for I have sinned. It is about two weeks ago since I came to confession."

The priest raised his hand reverently in a sign of the cross, and said something which pleased Kwesi. He was encouraged to divulge what was weighing him down mentally.

"I didn't keep the third commandment because I didn't come to church here. I rather went to a spiritual church with my mother and brothers and sisters," Kwesi said and paused. The Reverend Father waited a few seconds and asked in a distinct and very mellow voice,

"Anything more, my dear one?"

"No, not that I am aware of."

The father, not necessarily willing to lose a soul of his flock, said slowly,

"Your immediate idea to attend service on Sunday is commendable but beware of some of these small mushrooming churches with the self-styled prophets and prophetesses who are just in the institution for financial and other material gain," he said and continued with his admonitions and, finally, told Kwesi to make the act of contrition. The priest kindly gave him the needed absolution. An immense peace of mind descended on him and his satisfaction was rooted in the fact that he was going to do all he could to entice his mother and brothers and sisters, especially Kojo back, yes back to the Catholic Church.

CHAPTER 3

Some of the members of the spiritual church were sick people looking for a miraculous cure from the prophetess. Others were childless women who would do anything to see that they were pregnant. It didn't matter whether the process in getting this end meant seducing other women's husbands or better still the young male children of the prophetess.

As her church had achieved a respectable popularity, there were still others who were under training to become their own self-styled prophets and prophetesses. These personages were privileged in the church and usually sat in the reserved front pews. They were always decked out in white apparel with cross marks of white clay on the exposed parts of their body. These privileged personalities, especially the women, had a right to have all night prayer sessions with any of the handsome men of the congregation of their choice. Among the very horny male aspirants, one by the name Omane, had been assigned the job of praying privately with Araba.

Omane was neither handsome nor ugly although his presence and personality were striking. He was tall and slightly bow-legged. He had the habit of always gesticulating when he talked and he would always nod aggressively in acknowledging the affirmative. He was a fast talker and this habit of his delighted the prophetess for she could use him in many instances when she tried to make a point but couldn't. He was also left-handed.

There was something really pleasant about Araba that Omane liked immediately. Her pearly white and dark eyes were wide. Her face didn't even have a wrinkle after twelve children and she was tall and buxom. Her luscious lower lip hadn't seen deterioration since her former husband never kissed her.

Omane knew it was just a matter of time to seduce Araba as he had done to most of the women and was responsible for several pregnancies.

"Thank you prophetess for giving me Omane," Araba said modestly as she genuflected in front of the prophetess. She blessed Araba and said,

"Omane might be my heir if I should die soon. He is a good man."

True to her word, he was nothing else but a good gigolo. The relationship immediately cemented a bond of confidence among the three- the prophetess, Omane and Araba so that Kwesi's endeavor to lure his mother and brother back to the Catholic Church took a new tough turn. Araba was not only less keen on hearing her son talk about Catholicism, she was almost ready to disown him due to the prophetess and Omane's instructions.

Kwesi was flabbergasted at seeing his mother with Omane. He remembered Omane as the one who preached when he attended service with his mother and Kojo. Kwesi had immediately disliked him because he appeared too overbearing and rather too charismatic to be believed. Araba could see the indignation of her son but she dismissed it as mere child's folly.

"This is my new companion you must accept him and the new situation. Moreover, the prophetess says he is a good man," Araba told Kwesi.

"I thought you loved Papa so much that I didn't believe you would, so soon, go out with any man again," Kwesi said with wide-eyed amazement at his mother's words about Omane.

"A lonely woman needs a companion and don't get your mother wrong, I am not yet even forty years old even though I've had all these children.

"The prophetess says, the prophetess says… I don't believe that a woman can be God's messenger. Look at your former church; did you see a woman priest?"

"I didn't but Catholics are the most conservative male chauvinists. The pope and all his bishops and priests are liable to moral corruption. We are in a dynamic world and obsolete ideas must yield to revolutionary ones."

"Please have you considered marrying this future prophet or he is just a friend?"

"The prophetess had not talked about marriage yet but maybe it's in the pipeline. I will do what she sees fit for me."

"You are being dominated too much by the prophetess."

Her anger was evident in the two hard slaps Kwesi received on his right cheek. He turned silent.

Araba's love for Omane was not platonic. She immersed herself head over heels in Omane's love oblivious of any disappointment. Her love him waxed at the near fatal neglect of her children. In the meantime, she had instructed Kojo to go and stay with the prophetess who agreed to keep him. He served her so well that she put him in charge of the incense. She also assigned him to the bandsmen to train him in the playing of the trumpet. Soon he could play by ear three of the church songs.

His new position as the trumpet boy pleased his mother so much that she brought the prophetess very expensive gifts of gold ornaments accumulated through Omane's help. He himself had garnered them from some of the wealthier women and said that they would be a dowry for Araba. Omane didn't recognize what Araba had done until much later.

It was getting closer to Christmas. The prophetess had told her congregation that there would be a church harvest. The church members took the harvest time as an important occasion on which to display their wealth and extravagance. Some of them, the so called barren women, were pregnant, thanks to the clandestine activities of Omane and the connivance of the prophetess. No one knew where these women got their monies but they claimed their businesses had been flourishing and been very lucrative thanks to the generous spiritual succor of their beloved prophetess. Thus, they were the most charitable at these harvests.

November 20th was the appointed day for the harvest and with much anxiety, the prophetess prepared frantically for it. When the day came, there was pomp at the occasion.

Women dressed in elaborate silk clothes and weighty and shiny headgear. The prophetess didn't want to be outdone in extravagance so she was in an immaculate white silk material. She wore white gloves and shoes. She threw a white veil across her shoulders and needed two little girls to follow her while holding the superfluous material of her cloth behind her. The church was filled to the brim with people. First, there was the usual service and after that came the harvest. After some fat lady had bought the glass of water for ten million cedis, a heavily pregnant young lady went to the announcement system and said;

"I have longed to have a child. Now I am pregnant and my success is due to the munificent help of our prophetess. On account of this, I have not come to this august occasion empty-handed. I have an amount of eight million cedis to thank God and her." She had not finished yet, she continued,

"If I have a safe delivery and a girl, here, I add five hundred thousand cedis in advance in anticipation of that eventuality."

Kojo, who was listening attentively, suddenly took hold of his trumpet and blew high notes of one of the songs he had learned. Bedlam ensued. The congregation clapped, danced, and sang and brought their monies now and again to the collection barrel. This lasted throughout the song with very many refrains. Pretty soon, the prophetess' bell clinked and there was remarkable silence much in contrast to the pandemonium which had preceded it. She said,

"Your faith has brought you this far. Surely, you'll have a child and a daughter too according to your own hankering. Always drink the holy water. Use some to wash your face and stomach as soon as you get out of bed. My angels will be with you always to guide you through."

The heavily laden woman curtsied reverently as she said her "thank you."

The prophetess's ingratiating ability hit its maximum. For, many women and men came one after the other until the collection barrel was full of their money. An usher hurriedly took the barrel to a room at the back of the church where five elders were diligently counting the big pile of money. After the disposal of the money the usher rushed back with the barrel. That day, the church service and the harvest lasted deep into the night. When the total amount was counted, it was announced that they had collected thirty five million cedis. Incredible for this church. A renewed commotion only echoed from high notes Kojo blew. He sweated profusely and his constantly puffed cheeks assumed a rather different personality for him. At the harvest, the prophetess was decked out in outrageous ostentation. All the gold ornaments of Araba and Omane had been displayed over her white silk apparel with considerable pomp and emotion. Their intricate jewels apotheosized her image immensely. Omane was not happy when he saw this. He immediately nursed a heavy resentment in the deepest resources of his heart.

"These are my jewels," he said after considering whether to confront her. The prophetess said,

"These are Araba's gift in appreciation of my spiritual assistance to her. She claims business has increased four-fold through my prayers so she brought them to me as thanks."

"Well, they are mine and I want them back." Omane's forwardness astonished the prophetess for she had always considered him a subordinate, which he truly was. She was covetous of these ornaments and was not actually ready to release them to him.

Omane decided, there and then, that he was quitting the church. He was serious. Within a few days, he was nowhere to be found. His intentions were clear because he knew exactly what he was going to do. He was going to found his own church. As easy as that. With the help of some of the members of the prophetess's congregation whom he had been able to convince, he started a new spiritual church.

When the prophetess recognized what Omane had done, that he was drawing away people from her church, she called the attention of her congregation to a serious and wicked anathema on Omane. She predicted and cursed that in spite of the fact that Omane would succeed tremendously with his new church in terms of money and the number of his followers, he would suffer a most debasing death. He would die very young.

It was after the departure of Omane that goaded Kwesi on to try and get his mother and Kojo back to Catholicism and from the seemingly magnetic control of Araba by the prophetess. He argued that even the one who was the sole confidante of the prophetess had quit thus rendering the powers of the prophetess ineffective after all. Kwesi went through intermediaries but still saw little success.

Meanwhile, Kojo had been elevated to a new position of importance with the prophetess. She bought a Toyota Land Cruiser and handed it to Kojo for his sole keeping. He chauffeured her around wherever she wanted to go. His elation was beyond words.

"How would you like to be a future prophet under my own eyes and tutelage?" The prophetess asked Kojo after he had brought her home from a trip to town one hot and muggy afternoon. With a beaming smile Kojo said enthusiastically,

"Yes, the idea is fantastic, thank you."

"To be a full time student of mine you need to quit school and immerse yourself in this venture."

"But I will need certificates for my future security when it comes to job seeking."

"You think being a prophet is not a job?"

"Well…."

"Well what? You don't worry unnecessarily. I will let you in on this business. I could never build my church, a house and buy this beautiful car if I were not a prophetess. I just like you and Araba a lot and that is why I want to help you."

"I am really glad to hear that but I still think…."

"You still think what my dear boy? Don't you want to wield considerable power and be able to control people's mind on the question of salvation? There are many gullible people around, you know."

"Yes, I see people yearn for this thing which seems missing in their lives and are willing to pay any price for it," Kojo said and smiled contentedly.

"Look, you, as young as you are, have a very magnetic personality which appeals to my congregation. I always stand in awe whenever you pick up the trumpet. Immediately you blow your note, the whole church erupts into bedlam, excuse the word."

"So you think I can be a good prophet, your holiness?"

"Sure," the prophetess said with considerable emphasis.

"Thank you very much," Kojo said already won over, however, he could consult with Araba about it.

Araba was extremely happy that the proposal for Kojo had come up. First, it would relieve her of the immediate burden of continually looking after her son. It would be the prophetess's responsibility and why not!?

On the other hand, Araba always associated immense glamour with being a leader of a spiritual church and even thought about the fact that Kojo would someday be a leader of his own church and also make as much money as the prophetess.

"When does the prophetess want you to start?"

"I think she wants me to start immediately. Considering what she calls my magnetic personality, I do believe it will be a welcome news to all the congregation."

The following Sunday, the prophetess indeed called the attention of the congregation to this novel idea and proposal for Kojo. The idea was greeted with tumult. They clapped, sang, and danced approbation. Kojo, much encouraged, blew his trumpet hard. The prophetess asked for a collection to be used to support Kojo. After about twenty-five minutes of this rumpus the prophetess quieted them and announced,

"God has surely approved this already." There was instant loud applause.

"I see a strong prophet in Kojo so there will always be a special collection every Sunday for his support."

Araba couldn't believe her ears. The welcome message of hers on Kojo's behalf brought happy tears rolling down her cheeks. After the church service, she couldn't wait to go and thank the prophetess and still congratulate Kojo on his full acceptance by the whole congregation. All was set for Kojo's clerical education under the vigilant eyes of nobody but the powerful and dear prophetess.

For Araba, it looked as if going to college was being played back again because there was a new prospectus of items she must buy for Kojo before he went and joined the prophetess. Items included four white cassocks, two big and long rosaries, a cape and white hat-like headgear, white clay and two metal trunks.

On the fourth day of May, Kojo was in the premises of the prophetess to begin his training. His education included the art of divination, Spiritism and necromancy, black psychology, dream interpretation, occultism and church finance and of course some Bible knowledge. Despite incessant pleas of Kwesi about leading people astray and away from God as some spiritual church leaders were in the habit of doing, Kojo took no regard at all to his brother's pleas. All Kwesi could do was pray for his brother. However, anyway, despondency was getting the better of Kwesi as he thought that celestial intervention was proceeding too slowly for the transformation of Kojo and Araba back to the mother Catholic Church. Kojo, who was an under training prophet, was the coup-de-grace of all his efforts. What did Araba think? She thought Kwesi was too obstinate and disobedient. She said to him,

"Because of your stubbornness, you are always where you are. No progress. Look, Kojo is getting a good lead in life and, prospects for him in the future are definitely fantastic." Kwesi, toughened by previous life's experiences, said,

"What if I told you that I am also aspiring to become a Catholic priest?"

"Are you kidding, and not marry? You are doomed."

"I don't necessarily think so."

"Are you truly going to pursue it?" She bellowed out as if incredulous about it all.

"Yes, mother, I am, surely, decided. And won't you rather be the mother of a Catholic priest?"

"I didn't give birth to you to go take a vow of poverty. I need to be looked after in my old age."

"I am not your only child. Kojo, as you claim, will in no time be a prophet. You are aware of the monies such prophets make."

"Yes God's blessing be on my application at St. Hubert's Seminary. Later, I hope to be at the major Seminary at Pedu as well."

"Are you really serious son?" Araba was apprehensive.

"Yes, I am, mother." Kwesi didn't beat about the bush.

Araba's mind was not set at ease. She was not content that her own son, yes the eldest, was going to pursue such an abominable vocation as Catholic priesthood.

True to his word, Kwesi applied to St. Hubert's Seminary and secured a place at the school. He knew that the life span of a spiritual church was negligible as compared to that of the Catholic Church so he was sure he would finally succeed in winning his mother and brother over to Catholicism in the long run.

CHAPTER 4

There seemed to be contentedness in the air as Araba let her son, Kojo, immerse himself in his study with assiduity. She would always send Kojo the best of provisions to cushion the hardships of the times due to the stringent economic circumstances in the country. What of Kwesi? Well, he was a solitary seeker of God in the seminary. Araba never visited him nor sent him anything. Araba had not disowned him but she could have given him a better treatment.

Kwesi was always full of prayers and meditation for success in the long quest for the Catholic priesthood, and, also, for his mother and brother in their lostness for the same quest of Christian salvation.

Meanwhile, Omane's church, Faith Healing Church of God, was slowly taking root in Christendom. Omane, shrewd as he was, knew exactly what he was about because after having had tremendous experience as a Tro-tro and Neoplan bus preacher, a hospital and a marketplace preacher, not to mention the time with the prophetess, Faith Healing Church of God was indeed bustling. Many adherents came from all corners of Kumasi. The current talk of everyone was about Omane and Faith Healing Church of God.

"Have you heard of Prophet Omane?" asked one member.

"No, who is he?"

"Who is he?! You live in Kumasi and you haven't heard of Prophet Omane and his church. You must not be living here."

"Well, will you tell me who he is then?"

"Definitely. Go to Amakom and ask of Faith Healing Church of God. Everybody knows who he is by now. Not to mention the divine healing he is capable of, he is also very good in helping, business people of all walks of life.

"Are you a member?"

"Of course, I am. Can't you tell of my situation now? Where do you think all this money is coming from? You had better join it quick if you want any financial success."

"When is church service?"

"Sunday at nine in the morning and every day of the week at seven in the evening."

"You'll see me there tonight."

Omane had won yet another church member. Such was the proselytizing for him that his church grew in numbers day after day. After commanding a credibly good congregation, his motive became mercenary and thoughts of exploitation of his masses were a dominant theme in his mind.

"Look at 2 Corinthians Chapter 9 starting from verse 6. What does it say? It says, "Remember that the person who sows many seeds will have a large crop. Each one should give, then, as he has decided, not with regret or out of a sense of duty; for God loves the one who gives gladly. And God is able to give you more than you need for yourselves and more than enough for every good cause." "As the scripture says," Omane continued,

"He gives generously to the needy. His kindness lasts forever."

These verses were Omane's strongest and most important preaching statements. He had these verses memorized and could say them seven times in the same service.

He also referred to the widow's offering at St. Mark's Gospel Chapter 12 verse 42 to 44. The Widow's Mite. Yes. Omane attributed success in life to charity to God through manifestly large donations in church. Thus money was pouring in and his self-styled prophet hood took a new turn. Year after year, multitudes of people joined Omane's church and he had to make use of a public address system to reach out to his congregation. His church premises were soon found to be too small so a new and bigger building was underway. The members chipped in their labor and monies and soon there was this new transformation of Faith Healing Church of God into an outstanding edifice. Omane's name became a household word in Kumasi.

Progress in both schools of clerical education was going smoothly Kwesi performed excellently at St. Hubert's and Kojo was a dandy at the prophetess's church. After two years of unbroken training, Kojo got an occasional chance to preach and he was outstanding. Kwesi also finished the upper classes at St. Hubert's and he proceeded to Pedu Major Seminary. He now even wore the white cassock. After another year of vigorous attention by the prophetess, Kojo was ready for ordination into spiritual church prophet hood. There was pomp at the occasion. Araba was there with all manner of smiles and elation. After his symbol of authority, a whisk of horsetail, was given him by the prophetess, the whole church broke into their usual scene of noisy confusion of singing, clapping, dancing, and speaking in tongues. Despite Kojo's age, he had suddenly become a worshippable hero in all respects. He and his trumpet were ubiquitous in the church because he would preach his sermon and immediately after that blow his signature tune,

"Yesu Kristo ye kunim di frankaa." "Jesus is the victors' flagbearer."

After several years of being with the prophetess Kojo had been turned into another Omane much against his will.

"Your charisma demands that you have all night prayers with these women yearning for childbirth."

"Agreed, your holiness," said Kojo not knowing what it entailed. When he discovered the pleasures that went with male prophet hood he immersed himself head over heels into this diabolical misdemeanor. He was well paid for it because soon the prophetess bought a small private care for his use. Such awful behavior at the prophetess church was not to last forever because on Sunday the weakness of humanity came to a head. The prophetess had been giving her regular admonitions to those who were witnessing. Unfortunately for her she sank heavily into her chair and collapsed in an apparent spell. She was rushed immediately to hospital with Kojo driving the Land Cruiser as fast as he could. She was pronounced dead after a long battle to save her. After an autopsy, she was said to have had a massive heart attack. Her precipitate death took everybody by surprise. As dear as she was to her church, she was given an overelaborate funeral after she had been buried at a cemetery at Old Tafo. Her death was a big blow to her church and even Kojo, with all his charisma couldn't pull the church together as the prophetess had done. The church began to disintegrate not long after her death. She had died and her death also meant the symbolic obit of her church. Its dissolution epitomized in a rather grand way the actual life span of a spiritual church. Negligible.

The riddle and dilemma was solved for Araba concerning the prophetess's church and Omane's. In a conversation with Kojo, her motives were made evident.

"We've lost our prophetess and church as well. What do you think we should do?"

"I don't quite know. Back to Catholicism maybe."

"No, on my dead body. I have an idea. I think prophet Omane will surely welcome us in his new church."

"Fantastic!"

"With your experience as a trumpeter and a prophet, I don't believe he will hesitate to offer you a position in his church."

"Let's give it a try."

"We can go there even today," said Araba.

"O.K. I am ready anytime."

At the plush premises of Prophet Omane, Araba was the first to set the ball rolling.

"I beg you your worship, we've been old friends before and as you know old friends are more trustworthy than new ones."

"Get to the point," Prophet Omane said.

"Well, I want a place for myself and my son Kojo in your most flourishing church."

"Does Kojo still blow his trumpet?"

"Yes, I still do. I might say, I am even better now."

"He is also a good prophet," Araba cut in, "he received his ordination from the prophetess sometimes back before her death."

"Oh she died eh?" Prophet Omane said as if very astonished. Actually, he had heard about the prophetess's death through some members of his congregation but it looked as if he was hiding his contentment at her death.

"You are welcome to my church. To start with, Kojo can join the band and improve on it. I am aware of his capabilities at the trumpet."

"What about his job as a prophet?" asked Araba.

"That will come later. Exercise some patience."

"Thank you very much," Araba and Kojo said simultaneously.

With some tinge of sentimentality and good times of old, Araba asked,

"Am I still yours?"

"No."

Araba was taken aback and was instantly ashamed that she had asked that question. Her recent cheerfulness had turned into a dull indignation to even talk, but the prophet Omane broke the lull and said,

"I was only kidding. In fact I have a true lover's knot for you and I had missed you a lot."

Instantly, Araba was all smiles. Again she said,

"Oh is that so, thank you very much."

To display a bit of his opulence, Prophet Omane invited Araba and Kojo to dinner. It was a fantastic evening of sumptuous fufu and soup. There were four choices of soup, Nkatekwan, nkrakra, abekwan and abekatekonto. There were also beef, mutton, chicken, pork and turkey. With such an array of delectable nourishment, they all dug in with watering mouths after they had taken an appetizer of champagne. Yes, champagne!

"Mm good," said Araba.

"Thank you. I am always at your service," Prophet Omane said rubbing it in. after Kojo had taken another liberal swig of the wine, he remarked,

"Where do you get such good drinks?"

"Well, for your information, I have a very wealthy congregation some of whom travel abroad often for business purposes. Most of them have very good taste so they bring me such goodies from abroad. This drink came from France itself."

"I think we're in the right place," Araba said.

"Sure you are," Prophet Omane said rubbing it in again.

Kwesi's education had taken him to various places on the West African coast. He went to Gambia for a spell, stayed a couple of years in Liberia and now he was in Nigeria for some time. Thus getting to the end of his clerical training he was always away. Kojo kept in touch with him. However, he misinformed his elder brother of the true picture of the goings on with himself and their mother and certainly the country as a whole.

Once, Kwesi got a chance to visit Kumasi during his vacation. Araba was still not convinced that the Catholic priesthood was glamorous and better still a blessing from the Almighty. She said to Kwesi,

"I am not happy that my own son, yes the eldest, is always away from home."

"Mama, I am away for a very good reason. Isn't my absence a blessing to you? After all, I am being sponsored by the Reverend Bishop of the Kumasi Diocese and Amakom Parish."

"I know I am relieved financially but that is not the point. Being around me is more beneficial than the finances and support you talk about."

"But you've always thought that I am the black sheep of the family and you've even called me stubborn, obstinate and disobedient before. Why do you want a so-called mischievous son around you always?"

"A black sheep you are indeed. You are a very discernible member of this family."

"If you call me discernible as a mother, then, what do you think my future congregation will think about me?"

"Surely, they'll think likewise."

"Mama, to be able to convince you of this vocation of mine, which is a calling from God, it needs prayer. I will be earnest in praying for you and for your understanding. I will also let Kojo pray for you too.

"I will be gratified about Kojo's intercession and not yours because I know God will not listen to a disobedient son. You haven't gained anything from your career. Look at Kojo, in the short span of his prophet hood and ministry, he owns his own car and you are still walking.

"My vocation is not for material gain but for service to the people. In fact, I will soon take my vows of poverty and start on the salvation of my congregation and whoever will need my assistance in the spiritual vein."

This last statement set Araba's mind a-wandering. She said,

"What do you mean by taking a vow of poverty? I hope my son isn't cracking up." Kwesi did his best to convince and put his mother's limitedness in academic reasoning at ease but failed. This time she thought Kwesi also needed prayers from a spiritualist like Prophet Omane. Who else? Araba had previously told the prophet. He felt some condescension despite his own elevated status in his church. He, secretly, cherished the Catholic priesthood and was awed by the sanctity of it all much in contrast to spiritual church prophet hood. He knew that the last prophet of Christendom had come and gone and he also knew that modern day prophet hood was certainly misleading. He had even heard the Muslims saying that the Prophet Mohammed was the last of God's prophets. He was constantly baffled by his own lack of comprehension of his own prophecies because they always turned out to be false. Why is God treating his own prophet like this? He would ponder and ask.

Once, he had prophesied the impending end of the whole wide world. He claimed he had been inspired to make this pronouncement by a divine vision he had in a dream. Through his own expertise at dream interpretation, he had arrived at the pessimistic conclusion for all mankind not even sparing himself, a good prophet as he was. In the meantime, he had been able to convince his most gullible congregation, and most of them, the wealthy ones, had brought most of their wealth to the church and liquidated other property and come to a vigil at the Faith Healing Church of God to live out in great ostentation and extravagance the last lap of life. Why not? They indulged in gluttony, drank some good and spirituous liquor and engaged in unwarranted and outrageous carnality. For, as the recent theme of Prophet Omane went,

"Eat, drink and be merry for tomorrow you die."

Anxieties were high on the tenth of July, the day the prophecy would come true. That day indeed had some prophetic qualities for, no doubt, it rained and rained heavily. Raindrops were large and they fell heavily on the roofs and cause an apparent diabolical racket. For a long time it rained. The length of it really put fear in the congregation as they thought another rendition of the Great Flood of Biblical Times was at hand again.

Their fear was exhibited in their group praying but it was hard to discern what anybody was saying due to the constantly falling rain. Their fears were allayed because presently it stopped raining but praying continued and went deep into the night. The hours slowly ticked by and pretty soon, it was dawn the eleventh. The earth was still intact and nonchalantly alive and well. False Prophecy! Prophet Omane, to cover his embarrassment, insisted that their prayers had been heard by God and that the good Lord had spared humanity on account of his, Prophet Omane's intercessory prayer all night. Well gullible congregation, which did not want to put their beloved prophet to shame, swallowed Prophet Omane's assertion hook, line and sinker and held tenaciously to their prophet's new date which was ten years into the future. But will he, himself, live to witness the carrying out of yet another postponed prophecy?

After the disconcerting prophetic episode, prophet Omane sought to regain his tarnished image through Kojo's efforts, Kojo's magnetic personality had gained ground rapidly at the church. Although he could see through Prophet Omane's falsity, he agreed to enhance and perpetuate the prophet's teachings. He did extremely well and was rewarded by a new high position of assistant prophet only next to the church's most avowed and most infallible prophet.

Araba was highly ecstatic once again on her son's success, fame and the inevitable fortune. She prided herself on the fact that the whole top echelons of Faith Healing Church of God could be steered under her own authority. She was on good terms with his worshipful majesty, the highly elevated prophet of the true God and also none other than her own son, was, of course, assistant prophet, whatever that meant.

She designed schemes in her mind on how best to bring to bear her own influence on all from the lowest church member to the mighty prophet himself. What a shrewd illiterate!

CHAPTER 5

When Kwesi went back to Pedu, Araba was quick to travel to Anomabo and on to Cape Coast. At the premises of the seminary, Kwesi, who could not actually tell why his mother had come to his school unannounced, met her. Kwesi perceived his mother in a confused state at once and asked the reason why;

"I am here to see the authorities of the school," Araba couldn't help saying.

"For what, mama!" Kwesi's surprise was evident, and he raised his brows now and again, in complete amazement.

"What is my mother about?" he asked himself. Well, being nearly a priest, Kwesi was obliged to be most polite and courteous so he led his mother to the school's head's office. In his anxiety to know exactly why his mother was there, he asked her again and again. Araba, unlike herself remained calm and quite composed. Instead, she related briefly to Kwesi the goings on with Kojo and the prevalent state of affairs at home. The office was about four hundred meters from Kwesi's dormitory. They got there finally with anxieties running high in his thoughts.

As his thoughts wandered he suddenly came to grips with his vocation. Prayer. He, therefore, started to pray silently.

Reverend Father Oduro greeted the two with an infectious, cheerful smile. Kwesi smiled back. After the Reverend offered them seats, he made the sign of the cross and said a brief orison,

"Father, this is my mother," Kwesi said.

"Very nice indeed. You are most welcome here. Feel comfortable."

"Thank you."

"What can I do for you? Madam."

The niceness of father Oduro nearly made Araba desist from saying what she had on her mind but she began to talk.

"Kwesi has spent quite a bit of time here studying hard to become a priest. Upon considerable thought lately, I have come here to tell you and Kwesi that I don't want him to continue and become a priest after all."

"What, mama, did I hear you right?"

"Just be calm, Kwesi," the Reverend Father said.

"I am your mother and no matter how old you are, I am older and wiser. The Catholic priesthood won't be good for you at all."

"How have you come to this conclusion and why have you let me go so far into my studies, and now giving me such completely unexpected information?"

"Just be calm and let her go on, yes madam."

"I have had such malevolent dreams lately and one dream depicted Kwesi as a mere menace to his future congregation. In fact, he was so bad that he was stoned to death by some of his church members while on a retreat to Buoho."

"Can you believe that, Father? Superstition and nothing else," said Kwesi.

"Let her go on. I don't think she's finished, go on, madam."

"His own brother and another spiritual church prophet are very good at dream interpretation. I told them my dream and they came to the same conclusion that it was a very bad omen for Kwesi. I don't want my son to suffer unnecessarily."

"And these people said you should stop Kwesi?"

"Yes Father."

"Hmm," Father Oduro sighed heavily.

"Mother is too superstitious," Kwesi said.

"Be quiet. Whether I am superstitious or not is not the question here."

"There must be some other motives and not just the dictates of dreams as my mother is claiming."

"Well, yes!"

"Please what are they mama?"

"Oh about not marrying and about taking a vow of poverty?" Father Oduro said.

"You hit them right on the nail's head. I am still disturbed by them."

"Come on, mama."

"Wait a minute, Kwesi." Father Oduro said and hurriedly searched his pocket for a handkerchief because he was having a sneezing urge. The sneeze finally came and it was subdued and controlled. He wiped his nose with a very white handkerchief. He continued.

"Kwesi has spent a lot of time preparing for his ordination which will come soon, in fact, next July, to be precise. We have spent a good deal of money on his education and travels. Moreover, we believe that for anyone to be able to go this far is surely being called by God to this blessed ministry."

"Yes, I know he could be ordained anytime now. And that's the main reason why I am here. Don't forget the dreams, either, because I believe in them in too. Many people have witnessed in my church about dreams and according to them their interpretation came true always."

"Oh that's the point. Perhaps as you are a spiritual church member you want Kwesi to join you there too."

"Well, exactly, Father!"

"I in turn, want her and my brothers and sisters to come to the Catholic Church again. We were all members."

"Excuse me Father, but I think there is nothing to be gained in Catholicism except conservative ideas. The church has outlived its usefulness. New churches like mine in Kumasi are more revolutionary. However, I also don't believe that numbers of people in a church guarantee divine salvation."

"But, mama, you want me to stop my church and come to yours to swell your numbers as well. Aren't you still thinking about gaining more people to your church? I think you are envious of the following of Catholicism."

"Well, well, Madam, I think Kwesi has a right to choose his own career. He is interested in the priesthood and that's where his heart is. Why don't you pray for him instead? I am very sure that someday you will be very proud he became a Catholic priest. His personal ambition must hold sway here."

"Thank you, father," Kwesi said and beamed a toothy smile as if to think that Araba had been thoroughly convinced by Father Oduro.

"Madam, I know you'll be blessed abundantly if you allowed Kwesi to go on with his vocation and wait anxiously till July when your own son will be a fully ordained Catholic priest."

Araba sat motionless for a while and nodded her head aggressively. Father Oduro also nodded slowly and thought that Araba had understood the validity of his assertions. Araba asked leave to go as she realized that her mission had failed. A mission which was catapulted on her by the strong persuasiveness of who else but His most Reverend Holiness, the most avowed and most solemnly infallible Prophet Omane.

"God bless you, and don't ever stop praying for your son."

"I won't." She said finally. She undid her Dutch wax cover cloth and wrapped it more tightly around her waist. Kwesi was much immersed in meditative silence of thanks to God. Father Oduro led his mother out of the office. Kwesi saw her off as she took a taxi bound for Kotokoraba to take the bus back home to Kumasi.

Back home, Araba went straight to Omane's residence where she narrated what had gone on between her and the authorities and Kwesi at Pedu. Kojo, who had been absent from home finally came to Omane's residence as well.

"How did it go and how was my brother?"

"As you can see, your brother is not here with me. I couldn't convince them to get Kwesi to quit. Moreover, he has gone so far that taking him back will mean hurling himself off a cliff."

"I don't think brother Kwesi would have done that."

"As you know already Kwesi hasn't always obeyed my instructions. He forgets the commandment, honor your father and thou mother… yet he claims he is going to be a priest. What irony, a priest indeed!"

"So when is he going to become one finally. He has been in the seminary for quite a long time."

"Next July," they said.

"Next July!?" Omane who had left the room momentarily and had just returned asked.

"Yes," said Araba.

"Where will that be?"

"I am sure he'll be ordained right here at St. Peter's Cathedral."

"I suppose we should all be there," Kojo said.

"Not me," Omane said.

"Why not?" asked Araba.

"Because I have never been to a Catholic church before and I don't want to because I don't fancy having to kneel most of the time as I hear it done there."

Kojo first felt some joy in his heart but jealous the next, because of his brother's ordination. It is some years back since he deserted the Catholic Church and going there again meant to him an unexpected reunion he wasn't looking forward to but go he must definitely. This time he was determined to shed his prophet's cassock for ordinary clothes because he thought a priest's cassock was more dignifying than the prophet's.

July soon came around and Kwesi and nine other candidates were up for ordination.

"As the father sent our Savior Jesus Christ (John 8, 42), and the apostles and disciples were sent into the world by Christ our Lord, so priests invested with the same power as they, are sent daily for perfection of saints, for the work of the ministry and the edification of the body of Christ (Ephesians 4, 12)," the most reverend Bishop said and continued.

"The burden of this so great an office is therefore not to be imposed on anyone, but on those only, who, by sanctity of life, knowledge, faith and prudence can sustain it. Through your education of your life you are going to receive this high office." He continued,

"If anyone should have anything to say against them before God and God's sake, let him come forth and say it. Nevertheless, let him be mindful of his own state."

There was a pause after this. Araba consulted Kojo whether to spoil the whole thing for Kwesi and tell the Reverend Bishop and the rest of the congregation of Kwesi's disobedience to her on many occasions.

"No mama, don't say anything," Kojo said. The Reverend Bishop continued to admonish the priests-to-be. Finally, he said,

"Do preserve in your conduct the integrity of a chaste and holy life. Bear in mind what you do, be conformed in your lives to your ministry; and as you celebrate the mystery of the Lord's death, take heed that you take away your members from all vices and lust. Let your teaching be spiritual medicine to the people of God. By your preaching and example may you build up the church so that neither we many deserve to be condemned by God for promoting you to so high an office, nor you for receiving it, but rather, that we may be rewarded."

Kojo and Araba were much awed by the solemnity of the ordination. He felt a bit embarrassed about his own prophet hood yet he kept sitting, listening and watching.

As the Most Reverend Bishop knelt before the altar, the ordination candidates lay prostrate for the litanies to be recited. After this the Bishop rose, wearing a mitre and holding his crozier in his left hand. After some time all rose and Bishop and all the priests lay both hands on the head of every candidate who was now kneeling. The bishop finally said,

"Receive the power of offering sacrifice to God, and of celebrating mass, as well for the living as for the dead, in the name of the Lord."

"Amen," answered the newly ordained. The Bishop once again said,

"Do you promise me and my successors reverence and obedience?"

"I promise," the newly ordained priests said solemnly. During the last blessing by the bishop, he once again admonished them by saying,

"Endeavor to live a holy and religious life, and to please God Almighty, that you may obtain His blessings and grace which he will mercifully grant to you.

There was a general reception for the newly ordained priests and their families. Kwesi was quite anxious to learn from his mother and brother how the whole ceremonious event went. He asked,

"How did it go, mother of a priest?" He smiled.

"Quite fantastic, son," Araba also smiled.

"It was very solemn," Kojo, who couldn't help saying, contributed.

"Perhaps this might draw you closer to me and my church. Your own former church as well."

"No, don't count on me," Araba said.

"Me, neither," said Kojo.

Reverend Father Kwesi couldn't contain his surprise but he kept calm and composed and only smiled at yet his mother's and brother's obstinacy. However, he did not hesitate to invite them to his first mass on the following Sunday.

It was a bright and sunny Sunday morning, a few white clouds floated effortlessly across the sun producing occasional cooling shades. There was a constantly blowing breeze so that the early heat was not so terrible stifling. Revered Father Kwesi's mass was not to be said at the Cathedral but rather at the Amakom St. Paul's parish church. The parish priest, the acolytes and the congregation were all set for their new priest.

Father Kwesi felt some nervousness but as he followed the longer-than-usual line of choristers, amidst solemn hymns, his initial nervousness deserted him replaced by a most grand confidence. He got this after he had said a brief prayer and invoked on St. Stephen's (his patron saint's) help on this august occasion.

Araba and the rest of his household including Kojo were all there decked out in their Sunday best. Those members of the Amakom parish who recognized Araba were full of congratulatory approbation for her.

"In the name of, the Father, the Son, and of the Holy Spirit, Amen," Father Kwesi intoned in a deep, sweet baritone which richly filled every corner of the church through microphones. He blessed the water and started with the "Asperges me..." Araba and Kojo remembered old times (it had been a long time) and crossed themselves when the holy water was sprinkled on them. There was a touch of awesomeness as Father Kwesi did it. After this, he continued flawlessly with the rest of the mass which was highlighted by the vociferous and well-meant sermon. Most of the congregation partook in the communion and Father Kwesi was overjoyed that he became a priest. Araba was finally proud of her son but would she join him?

CHAPTER 6

Araba elaborated on her narrative of Father Kwesi's ordination to Omane who deliberately refused to be impressed. He hated Catholicism not because the church lacked spiritual ministration. His church was sizable but he wished for a much larger following just like in the Catholic Church. To Araba, in whom he confided, such thoughts were only wishful thinking.

"We must be building another church," Omane said to Araba.

"Are you thinking about expanding already?"

"Well, why not!"

"In another suburb of Kumasi or somewhere else?"

"Not here, exactly."

"But where?"

"I am thinking about the rural areas, Bekwai, for example."

"Are you sure those people have heard about the church?"

"I am with you always but you have no eyes. Don't you remember when I introduced a delegation from that town at one of our Sunday church services?"

"You remember I left for Cape Coast to visit Kwesi at Pedu. I could be then that they came."

"You are quite right. I am sorry I never told you about it. Actually I am going to expand."

"Good luck, dear," she said and smiled.

"Kojo can take charge of the fledgling church at Bekwai and build it up and I know he can do it too."

"That's very welcome news indeed. But I don't think he can do it."

"I have discussed it with Kojo and he is very excited about the whole thing. I am surprised he didn't tell you about it. But why do you say he can't do it. Don't you have confidence in your own son?"

"He lacks your prophetic presence," she said this to see Prophet Omane's reaction. All that Araba was getting at was that she wanted Kojo to be in Kumasi for there was more money to be made in a big city than in a smaller town.

"Kojo has a magnetic and charismatic personality through which I have elevated him to this lofty position of assistant prophet and he has done marvelously well. I think he can do it."

"I don't want my son to be in a small town," Araba sounded a bit blunt."

"Where do you want him?"

"Here in Kumasi, of course."

"Venal motives, I guess."

"Well, yes, isn't it why you are also in Kumasi?"

This statement suddenly annoyed Prophet Omane for he didn't want anybody, not even a good friend like Araba to point out his faults and personal ambitions. But obviously, he was in the religious business for money and status because the following Sunday he, cursorily, announced to his congregation that he needed a new more luxurious car. To the congregation it was only a cursory remark but deep down in Prophet Omane's heart, he meant it because he again and again jokingly reminded the church members until they all agreed to establish a special first collection towards a fund for purchasing the car.

Prophet Omane actually had his eyes on the latest Mercedes Benz car. He wished the church could satisfy this desire to coincide with his birthday that year. True to his wishes, the church purchased the Mercedes for their dear prophet in late November. To advertise himself and the car, he soon called for a convention. It was also going to be a healing crusade as he called it.

Many people were obviously going to be present and there the Mercedes Benz would surely help to magnify the honorable personality of his most high, dedicated and infallible, true prophet directly chosen by God.

The convention went well. It was close to Prempeh Assembly Hall. Many women decked out in white cloth and headgear converged from every corner of the country. There were close to six thousand people present. As it had been broadcast about that it was also a healing crusade and psychotics, epileptics, schizophrenics, hunch backs and midgets had been taken there in their numbers. There were also the lame, the blind and deaf and people with speech problems.

In fact, there were healings and one would wonder whether, in all verity, they were genuine ones. For, a man who claimed to be deaf and speechless and who was quite expert in sign language gave a too-good-to-be-true witnessing much to everybody's amazement. His fluency in the Akan language could only be likened to the sweet language of Okyeame Akuffo and, a once deaf and speechless person, his tongue newly loosened, was speaking impeccable Twi and proverbs to boot. Wonderful indeed!

Everyone was waiting for the chance when that very crazy man was going to be healed. Prayers were said but when Prophet Omane realized that all invocation on the name of Jesus was proving futile, he announced that the man was possessed by the devil and that he needed private prayers. Poor Prophet Omane. The crazy man was not seen again during the rest of the convention. Piteous man. During the convention collection was taken six times a day. Why not? People were willing to pay so prophet Omane was also ready to collect.

What also could beat the shrewd manner of Prophet Omane's thinking? Among the congregation of Faith Healing Church of God were selected teenagers who did serious business for the church. Araba had been chosen to organize these teenagers. What they did was sell church T-shirts, writing pads, fountain and ballpoint pens, visors and other souvenirs. Prophet Omane also got Araba to prepare food items, which she sold to those at the convention. Her acumen at trading enabled her to make a lot of money indeed. The whole convention was a very successful financial triumph for, after the six days, an amount of three hundred and fifty million cedis had been collected excluding Araba's and the teenager's business. Not bad for an average of about fifty million cedis a day. Wow!

On the last day of the convention, one man's witnessing could have spoiled the whole success of it. He stood in front of the crowd and condemned the whole healing episode. He said that everything was a hoax and many of the healings had been planned beforehand. He insisted that there were too many afflicted people in the hospitals and if these prophets really cared, they were there that needed help. All at once, Prophet Omane got the microphone and told the congregation that the man was seriously deranged and therefore needed prayers. The man struggled to refute Prophet Omane's allegation but he was whisked away before he could do any more damage to the prophet's standing in the whole convention.

Ironically, the main theme of Prophet Omane's six-day sermon was the iniquity of irresponsible sex. He could quote a lot from the Bible to prove the wrongness of illicit sex as if the recurring theme was the only thing he sought from the Holy Book. He said,

"Second Corinthians Chapter 12 verse 21 states,

"I shall bewail many which have sinned already and have not repented of the uncleanness and fornication and lasciviousness which they have committed."(KJV)

Galatians Chapter 5 verse 19 states,

"Now the works of the flesh are manifest, which are these: Adultery, fornication, uncleanness, and lasciviousness."(KJV)

"Note that fornication is a sin because the Lord himself says at 1st Corinthians Chapter 6 verse 13,(KJV)

"Now the body is not for fornication, but for the Lord and the Lord for the body." Getting down to the same 1st Corinthians at Chapter 5 verse 18, the Bible states,

"Flee fornication…he that commits fornication sins against his own body."(KJV)

"In fact, I call upon you to read the whole 1st Corinthians book because at chapter 6 verse 9, also, Paul tells us that,

"Do not be deceived: Neither the sexually immoral nor idolaters nor adulterers nor male prostitutes shall inherit the kingdom of God. (NIV)

"Even at Hebrews Chapter 12 verse 16 Paul continues to exhort us that,

"See that no one is sexually immoral…"(NIV)

"The Bible still teaches us to

"Flee youthful lusts" (2 Timothy @, 22)(KJV)

"I believe that from all these examples from the Holy Book you'll all agree with me that illicit sex is a sin much against the will of God. Guard against the evil enticer. The woman who wears perfume, which excites the sense of smell and wiggles her backside in an attempt to seduce others, is surely the devil. Let her not do that and be devilish."

Yet, in the congregation of Faith Healing Church of God, there was a very beautiful adolescent girl. She was prudish, quite innocent and a virgin. A new dimension of desire had crept into Prophet Omane and he dreamed of seducing the innocent virgin. His conscience gnawed at him but,

"What the heck, I will do it and repent later," he said.

Prophet Omane couldn't sit to see Serwaa's breasts develop into nice protuberant pear shapes so one evening after church service, he called her,

"Serwaa."

"Yes, holy prophet."

"Don't call me holy prophet."

"O.K. SOFO!"

"Don't call me SOFO either."

"But you are a preacher, aren't you SOFO then?"

"Yes I am a preacher in church but outside the church I am like any other person just like you."

"Oh, is that true?"

"Yes, it is very true."

Serwaa smiled and Prophet Omane knew he had driven his point home but now came the crucial "bossing" of the young virgin.

"Did you come to church alone today?"

"No, I came with my mother but she says she is in a hurry so she left for home before the service was over."

"Take this Bible to the mission house for me."

"Sure, I will do it immediately."

Almost all the church members had dispersed. Prophet Omane engaged a couple of them in very short conversations, dismissed them quickly and furtively followed Serwaa. Serwaa was just coming out of the door when the prophet asked her to do another favor for him. After Serwaa had done it, he gave her a crisp five hundred cedi note. Unsuspecting Serwaa was very excited indeed and giggled pleasurably.

"Thank you, Sofo."

"I told you not to call me Sofo, didn't you hear?"

"Oh, I forgot, sorry."

"Serwaa, go to this room and bring me a pillow from the bed. I want to relax in the living room for a while."

Prophet Omane switched on the fan and turned on the television and quickly tiptoed into the bedroom and, in an innocent manner, she complied.

"Serwaa, let's talk."

"I beg you about what? Actually, I must go."

"You are very beautiful. Don't go so soon."

"Oh, is that so? Thank you. Just ten minutes."

"I like you very much. In fact, I like you so much that I will give you another five hundred cedis. Don't show the money to your mother when you get home."

Prophet Omane produced the money and Serwaa eagerly grabbed it. She had never had so much money and this ploy of the prophet really excited her. He didn't have to beat about the bush anymore to be direct and forward. He said,

"Will you give it to me?"

"The money, but you just gave it to me."

"Not the money."

"But what should I give to you. You know I don't have anything."

"Every girl has something she can give to a man," Prophet Omane said this and gingerly brushed Serwaa's left breast which he claimed a mosquito was biting. Serwaa suddenly realized what her prophet was about and missed a heartbeat. After that her heart started pounding.

"I beg you, I must go."

"No, but you just came here."

"Oh no, I must really go."

"Haven't you done it before?"

"No, leave me," and she began to sob.

"The first time I met Araba, she already had six children, but when I asked her whether she did it before, she said no," the prophet joked.

Serwaa thought it was an expensive joke so she stood up to go. Prophet Omane pulled her down instantly. When she realized what the prophet was getting at she was crying unceasingly. Prophet Omane managed to remove her dress and pull down her panties and lay her on the bed. He gagged her and held her down with his left hand. He frantically undressed himself.

Just when he was about to go down on her there was a loud knock on the door and immediately, and with a pounding heart, he sought to put his clothes on. The knock increased in intensity. He tried to shush Serwaa from her loud sobbing lest somebody hear her. His luck came from the noise of the television.

"Prophet Omane are you there?" From the voice, Prophet Omane easily knew that it was Araba.

"Ehe," said Serwaa.

He begged Serwaa to get under the bed but she refused. Araba was impatient for, she knew the prophet was at home. Usually, he never went anywhere after church service. Moreover, she could hear the television running.

After Prophet Omane had been able to persuade Serwaa finally to go under the bed, he hid the rest of her clothes and quickly went to the door. With a brief inspection of himself, he slowly and gingerly opened the door.

"Oh, it's you Araba."

"Yes, but why the delay? I've been knocking for quite a while. You should turn down the T.V. it is too loud."

The prophet did so and quickly asked her 'amanee.' She gave it. It happened that she had gone home and a neighbor had brought a child who was having seizures. She told the child's mother that she could bring the child to Prophet Omane. The mother, aware of the popular name of the prophet, allowed Araba to bring her child for ethereal prayers. So here she was with the baby.

Prophet Omane cleared his throat and almost dismissed them by saying that he could see the baby was well after all.

"Oh, do something for the little child. A little prayer maybe."

"I am not very well now and I was about to sleep. Doesn't the bed look slept on? Come and see."

"Yes, but prophet, you should think more of the other person than your own comfort. I need not tell you this. Have pity on the child."

All attempts by the prophet to get Araba to leave failed. Therefore, he was forced to start an erratic prayer for the child. The prayer show he put on surprised himself.

Meanwhile, because of the lowness of the bed and the very awkward and uncomfortable position Serwaa was in, she sought to relieve herself of the discomfort for at least a second. While at it, she made a noise, which pricked the ears of Araba. Serwaa's leg and knocked against something under the bed.

"You must have rats in your room because I can hear strange noises coming from under your bed."

"Oh you heard noises eh? These rats really worry me. I am out of pesticide and I will purchase some soon. I don't know how they get there. I'll be sure to kill all of them."

The noise persisted, for, Serwaa was getting exhausted from her awkward position. Araba, who had fear of mice and rats, went straight to the bed and lifted the wooden structure and let it down again.

"Agyei," cried Serwaa due to the sudden strong pain.

"Did I hurt somebody there? I thought I heard the cry of a person."

A pained "NO" came from the shaking lips of the prophet and an agonized "yes" came from under the bed.

Araba knelt to take a look under the bed and there was this big human "rat" under it.

"Shiee! Serwaa, what are you doing here? Come out, come out quickly."

Serwaa came out from under the bed almost naked except for her panties and underskirt. Araba was not a child. She could tell that there was something fishy about the whole God forsaken deal so she just sat in a pensive mood and didn't ask any questions. Everything was so obvious.

Prophet Omane begged her to keep quiet about it. To make sure, he asked her and Serwaa to swear on the Bible that they wouldn't say a word about this embarrassing situation.

They both agreed and swore not to say a word and the prophet was quite satisfied, at least, for the moment. What excited Araba was that she had got grounds for blackmail. Serwaa, despite her age, was thinking along the same lines. Poor Prophet Omane, why did he think an opportunity to deflower a virgin was a good thing? Of course, as a responsible church leader, certainly, he should have known better and stop playing with fire. His embarrassment was very profound indeed.

CHAPTER 7

Kojo went to Bekwai to lead the branch of Faith Healing Church of God and, as astute as Araba was, she was able to blackmail Prophet Omane into buying a truck for Kojo.

With money mania in mind, Kojo took advantage of the government's call for the production of exportable none traditional food crops like ginger, avocado pear, pineapple, oranges and lime, sugar cane and mangoes by farming. He also had hopes for cash cropping cocoa and coffee but that was a bit of a fantasy now.

For labor, why not use the exploitable labor force of the church? On many Sundays, he preached about the absolute necessity of hard labor for God and the Faith Healing Church of God, at least, one or two days a week. He gave "Kofi and Ama" a new meaning. He maintained that the usual "Kofi and Ama" collection was not enough; he preached that every member of the church would contribute labor, at least, once or twice on the day he was born. Kojo insisted that hard work for Christ was the same as fasting and that God favored those who also worked hard for the church.

His future plans made him like a slave master for, he intended to work the members hard when they turned out in their numbers to work. He finished his preaching by saying,

"If you want to work hard for Christ, clap your hands."

They all clapped for who wouldn't want to work for the Lord. Everybody wanted to.

"Adwuma," (meaning "work" in the Ashanti language), he said.

"Yebeye," "We shall do it"

"Adwuma pa. Adwuma denden" (Hard work)

"Yebeye."

"If you really want to work for Christ then clap your hands again."

The congregation clapped louder than before.

"God bless you, God bless you. We shall all indeed be in paradise."

"Praise the Lord."

"Alleluia"

"Paradise"

"We shall be there"

"Paradise"

"We are there already."

Kojo was happy that he had his congregation under his arms so he didn't hesitate to contact the chief of Bekwai. A large expanse of land was put at his disposal. Every Monday, Kojo and Adwoa, these born Monday worked on the land clearing bushes and cutting trees. The same thing happened for those born on Tuesday and it followed like that till Saturday. Sunday was declared a day of rest after church members had vehemently disagreed with their prophet to let Kwesi and Esi, born on Sunday, to work after church service. Therefore, those born on Sunday were put to work with those working on Saturday. Thus was the roster, which was thought out by farsighted Prophet Kojo.

It all happened by some weird coincidence that Father Kwesi was also posted to Jakobu a village near Bekwai. He had become the parish priest of the Jakobu parish. Rev. Kwesi also worked very hard and in only about a year and a half he had built a kindergarten and a junior secondary school for the villagers. His work was based on the social commitment and upliftment of the standard of the people.

Upon his advice and financial support, they dug wells and boreholes to improve the quality of the village's drinking water. His work was not just centered at Jakobu but also the outlying villages including Bekwai. In a short time, the two names of Prophet Kojo and Father Kwesi were on everybody's lips. Unlike Prophet Kojo's mercenary motives, Father Kwesi's motives were on the lines of true genuine altruism. He was the epitome of a true, honest preacher, teacher and social worker who combined sound Christian teaching of honesty, patience, humility, charity, love and integrity with social work in the villages to provide some of their needs. He was thus a true and ideal representative and symbol of Catholicism.

Prophet Kojo highly respected the excellent theological knowhow of Father Kwesi. He valued him for his erudition and wished he could learn from him. When they met, Prophet Kojo said,

"How would you like me to visit you for Sunday school? Not necessarily on Sundays because I have my service to conduct."

"That means you should come on Saturday when I will be ready for Bible discussions." Father Kwesi said this hoping to pull the prophet a step more towards Catholicism.

"We are all preachers and how do you expect me to come to your church before I go to conduct my service. Don't you know it will by hypocrisy? Have you ever seen a Moslem going to church on Sunday and then to the mosque to worship Allah? I can't do what you are saying."

"Do you actually know the Bible?"

"Of course, but don't tell anyone I was learning the holy book from you."

"Saturday then," said Father Kwesi. Kojo had two vehicles and Father Kwesi just had a motorcycle. He had his farms while Father Kwesi had none. Why should he leave all these things and return to Catholicism?

"It is obvious because what you want me to do will just as well undermine my prophet hood and status in my church."

"Well, you brought the idea, not me." For the sake of brotherhood and an attempt to help Prophet Kojo help others in the spiritual realm, Father Kwesi agreed to Tuesday and Thursday afternoons. This was top secret between them. After several weeks of intense biblical education under his brother, Prophet Kojo wanted to pay his brother by bringing him foodstuff after every harvest. Father Kwesi courteously declined to take them. He knew how Prophet Kojo had been exploiting his church members and, of course, many persuasions for him to stop had failed.

Araba had Prophet Omane come often to visit Prophet Kojo and Father Kwesi for he was uncomfortable somehow about his own hypocrisy and he thought that, direct meeting would be tantamount to a juxtaposition of hypocrisy and integrity. The prophet, therefore, wanted none of that. They drove to Kojo's place where Kojo drove Araba to Father Kwesi's premises at Jakobu.

"You are getting fat Kojo." Araba said about her son.

"Can I guess it's good living?" Prophet Omane said and nodded vigorously while smirking.

"Of course, what else?" Araba said, also smiling.

"There's an immense peace of mind that prevails within the church and I am doing well here. The barren are bringing forth, the farmers are getting bumper crops, the sick are healed; the spiritual succor is everywhere at Bekwai."

"Praise the Lord."

"Alleluia," both Prophet Omane and Araba said aloud.

"How about the farms? How are they doing?"

"Fantastic."

"I believe it's a very good business venture. But I must say headquarters in Kumasi wants a share of the booty." Prophet Omane was quick to point out.

"Why, prophet, it was his own hard work. Why should you think of taxing him?" Araba asked.

"Don't forget it's because of my church and name that Kojo is here and doing well."

"I know but even the government does not tax you!" Araba said.

"No, why should they? Our institution is ecclesiastical," said Prophet Omane.

"Then forget about taxing my son." Prophet Omane wanted to insist but stopped because Araba was always reminding him of the encounter with Serwaa. Because of this, Prophet Omane always kept quiet.

Meanwhile, the cook of Kojo was preparing an exquisite meal of fufu and mutton and chicken soup to welcome his elder prophet and his mother; he also served beer and other soft drinks. He did not want to outdo his prophet who served champagne and other exotic drinks at every meal. This trio was really living it up in spite of somber economic hardship in the country. Truly, founding a spiritual church was certainly not out of place at this time because some of the prophets could always play on the weakness, ignorance and the gullibility and vulnerability of their congregation to have a very ostentatious and high standard of living. Prophet Kojo always preached about the transfiguration of Christ and the fact that while Jesus was displaying just a tiny bit of his glory to come he also talked about his suffering on the cross. So Prophet Kojo told his congregation always,

"No cross, No crown."

Glory must be preceded by suffering and with this preaching his congregation accepted that they must keep quiet about their suffering and work hard because man's happiness was not mundane and paradise awaited everybody who suffered on earth. He always said his good living was justified because as a prophet he was ministering and getting people closer and closer to the almighty.

After a protracted time of relaxation and conviviality, Kojo took Araba to Father Kwesi and Jakobu. Father Kwesi, as usual, was very happy to see his mother.

"How is it, Father?" Araba asked.

"By God's grace, I am fine. Thanks to him. How about you?"

"Can't complain, Father."

"I have been visiting Father," said Kojo

"That's good of you," said Araba.

"In fact it was he who explained in detail some of the bible chapters and verses. I had never understood the significance of our Lord's transfiguration, but his explanation really enlightened me," Kojo said.

"You mean you are a prophet and you don't know the Bible well?" Araba tried to pull the leg of her son. They all laughed and thought it was a good joke.

It was at this visit that Kojo disclosed his intention to get married to one of the daughters of the chief of Bekwai.

"I am so glad for you," said Father Kwesi. "God is blessing you," he continued.

"I am very glad too. It's about time I have a grandson or granddaughter," Araba said.

"When is the marriage taking place?" Father Kwesi asked.

"Very soon. I have already given the "knocking" drinks. I want to give a big bride price to the chief for him to know that I am a very capable man."

"I can foresee a grand wedding at Bekwai already. By the way, what church does she belong to?" Father Kwesi asked his brother.

"When I came to Bekwai, she said she was an avowed Catholic. One day a friend of hers invited her to my church and right there she became attached to me and my church."

"Surprising how people just decide to leave the Catholic Church," Father Kwesi said.

"The Church has nothing to offer," said Araba.

"Let's not go into that again. Time will only tell which church is good or bad. The Catholic Church came since Peter in spite of many of the attempts of many of its original members who turned dissident to spoil it. They haven't succeeded yet and they never will," Father Kwesi was quick to say. "Someday, I hope some of these people will surely not have fulfillment in this proliferation of churches and will eagerly return to the mother church. I always pray for that."

"What's your wife-to-be's name?" Araba asked to change the subject.

"Yaa Donkor. Her father calls her Yoonko affectionately."

"Let us in on the date of the wedding. For the first time I will visit you in your church. Bring Yoonko here for a visit." Father Kwesi said.

"Yes do that Kojo, I am looking forward to that day," said Araba.

Kojo suddenly looked at his watch and realized how long he and his mother had stayed at Father Kwesi's residence.

"What time is it?" Araba asked.

"It's nine twenty. I don't think you can leave tonight with Prophet Omane. Why don't you stay overnight with me?"

"Don't forget that we have a Mercedes Benz. You know how it performs. I am sure Prophet Omane will want us to leave for Kumasi. He wouldn't want to miss service tomorrow," Araba said.

Kojo and his mother didn't dilly-dally any longer and they said goodbye to Father Kwesi who had thoroughly enjoyed their company. They stood up to go.

On their way back to Bekwai, Kojo couldn't help but disclose exactly what he had heard of his brother.

"People at Jakobu really love my brother."

"I could sense that," Araba said.

"They say he leads such a good and exemplary life that in Jakobu alone, people are stemming the drift from Catholicism to spiritual churches. I have heard he is so unselfish that people throng his church just to hear him preach."

"Visit him often and learn a good deal from him to improve the quality of your life and preaching. There is much to be gained from Bekwai. After the wedding, think about where you'll put up and raise a family. You must build a house in Kumasi by all means."

"Yes that's very true. Has Prophet Omane talked about building anyway? Why don't you get him to start building for you? After all he gets a lot from you."

Soon they were in Bekwai and Prophet Omane queried them about why they had kept him waiting for so long. Araba apologized because she and Kojo did not have any good reason. The spiritual church trio talked about Kojo's marriage and building plans despite the fact that it was really getting late. Prophet Omane and Araba finally hopped into the Benz and drove off into the silky darkness to Kumasi in about twenty minutes. Araba stayed at Prophet Omane's and went to bed with him. A prophet with a girlfriend! Wow!

CHAPTER 8

It was an august ceremony at the wedding. The birds had sung, the sun was bright, the morning air was cool and fresh and Prophet Kojo and Yoonko were dazzling and beaming smiles. It happened on the second Sunday of July and almost the whole of Bekwai was at the church. Father Kwesi, always fervent in prayer and overflowing in charity, brought kind gifts to his brother. Prophet Omane and Araba were, of course, also present. The chief and his retinue had all come in royal dignity.

Instead of local traditional clothes for a marriage ceremony Kojo was outfitted in a navy-blue tuxedo. It was an elaborate wedding never seen or heard of in the whole history of Bekwai. People thronged the place so much that the ostentation and extravagance of the occasion were on the lips of many a Bekwai citizen for very long years.

Prophet Omane had been accorded the privilege of officiating at the wedding. He outdid everyone in materialistic presence because instead of his usual white cassock he also wore a maroon tuxedo with a gold-pinned spotted tie, jelly curls and a diamond-studded gold ring. The parked Mercedes and very many other cars of guests of honor brought dignity to Kojo.

Araba was, of course, not to be left out in the solemnity of the occasion. She wore a yellow and blue kente camisole and cloth. Her hair was permed and curled nicely. She had a longer-than-usual elaborate gold chain, which almost reached her navel. Her earrings and bracelets were also gold. Her awesome presence only suggested an added flair to her involvement in a spiritual church. After all, where was she getting the money from if not from Prophet Omane and Kojo? "Found a spiritual church if you want to live in grand style," so the current saying went and it was true. Accompanying Prophet Omane and Araba were three busloads of some of the congregation of Faith Healing Church of God of Kumasi. They came with all kinds of gifts.

The church in Bekwai was smaller than that in Kumasi but there was a wide expanse of land just in front of it so, prior to this wedding ceremony, a huge shed had been erected. The immense shed was filled to the brim and there was standing room only.

The wedding itself went well. Everything was a copycat Catholic wedding interspersed with the usual spiritual church racket of loud drumming and dancing. Kojo was specially invited by Prophet Omane to blow his trumpet to delight those present and he did so marvelously well that all the people of Bekwai and Kumasi stood in awe of him. Yoonko was thus very proud of her husband. After the wedding, a grand reception followed. Savory bowls of rice and beef, chicken or mutton were served. There were many different types of drinks also. The sophisticated exotic drinks were served to the important guests including the chief. There were abundant soft drinks and locally prepared "elewonyo" for all. For musical entertainment, Agya Koo Nimo came with his mellifluous voice and percussive rhythm. The newlyweds got many nicely wrapped plates and cutlery which could last ten years. All the rest of the presents could fill a couple of rooms. Although Kojo didn't need all this head start because of his wealth, Yoonko was ecstatic. After a long period of merry making, the Kumasi guests left and the rest dispersed around nine o'clock at night.

Kojo and Yoonko stayed for a day's rest at Bekwai and took off for Kumasi on their way to Novotel in Accra for their honeymoon. Whose idea was this stay at the excellent French hotel with their gourmet dishes? It was all Prophet Omane's idea. Once the prophet had taken some church women in Accra for a midnight prayer session and baptism on the sea-shore. After finishing his mission, he entertained some of the women at the hotel. The incredible impressions on him led him to suggest Novotel to Kojo and Yoonko.

The couple had a classic and deluxe honeymoon. They lavishly tipped the waiters and waitresses. For this reason everybody wanted to be at their service.

Yoonko, a country girl, was not used to such extravagance even though she was the daughter of a chief. However, her extreme enjoyment of that microcosm of France and the noticeable wealth of her new husband compelled her to suggest,

"Why don't we take a trip to where all this comes from?"

"You mean to France?"

"Well, yes."

"No problem at all," Kojo said delighted that his bride was having a good time. To give Yoonko a treat since she was already talking about a trip Kojo said,

"Why don't we go back to Kumasi by plane?"

"Are you serious?"

"Yes, I never lie!"

"That's very nice of you because I never thought I would ever be in an aeroplane but this opportunity shouldn't be missed," Yoonko said with a lot of new contentment.

"I haven't flown before either and I am looking forward to this the day after tomorrow," Kojo said.

An attendant of the hotel helped Kojo and Yoonko get tickets for their plane trip. A taste of a foreign trip was right here with the couple beginning from Accra. Even more excited was Yoonko who, whenever she went to Kumasi, went to the airport of the metropolis just to see an airplane take off. Traveling in one was a dream come true.

They were on the plane the next day. When the plane suddenly jolted them backwards to start taxiing for the flight, Yoonko was suddenly afraid. It gained acceleration and she felt they were airborne. There was a weird surge in Yoonko's stomach and ears that made her panic a bit because she revealed her country upbringing by the way she held tightly to the seat in front of her. Kojo realized this and reassured her that everything would be alright although he himself was also panicking. The plane gained and gained height. After it had stabilized at a satisfactory height above the clouds, Yoonko dared to look out of the window and was suddenly very afraid. The whole episode was enervating for her because she had always had fear of heights. She felt like getting sick and would not unbuckle her seat belt even though she could see people do it. Even Kojo had gone to the back of the plane to ease himself.

"Are you sure you want to go to France?" Kojo asked teasingly.

"We can always go by boat."

After she said this, the plane suddenly took a descent.

"Agya ei," Yoonko shouted.

Kojo was getting embarrassed because some of the passengers turned to look at her and laughed. She held Kojo tightly till the descent ceased and the plane stabilized again. The episode repeated itself and became worse when the plane was finally in Kumasi and took a gradual descent for landing.

"What an uncouth girl," he thought.

"Take it easy Yoonko. It is also my first," he continued.

"I am so scared," she said.

Luckily for Yoonko and Kojo, the tires of the plane suddenly gave a screeching sound on the runway. Yoonko was holding Kojo's arm tightly until it taxied to a stop. She heaved a heavy sigh of relief. Kojo was also relieved.

They took a taxi and stopped at Hotel Saint Patrick on the Akorem road, for a brief relaxation and some cool drinks for it was a hot and muggy afternoon. After their relaxation, they were at Prophet Omane's residence. The prophet was all stretched out under a mango tree enjoying a breeze and reading The People's Daily Graphic.

"Oh, how are the lovebirds?" the prophet said and got up to shake their hands while talking as fast as he could and gesticulating wildly.

"We are fine, and you?" Kojo asked.

"Just fine, my dear, thanks. Araba was here with me but she just went to attend to some business. She said she'll be right back."

"O.K." said Kojo.

Yoonko had been too shy to talk. She didn't want to remember the flight and Kojo wished both of them never did but he held Prophet Omane in conversation about Accra and Novotel.

"How did you find it there?" the prophet asked.

"Very well, we just enjoyed ourselves. We enjoyed ourselves so much that when Yoonko asked where the original place of the hotel was and she was told France, she wanted us to take a trip there."

"I have thought of it often myself. France will be such a place for tourism and entertainment." Yoonko was smirking and said,

"You can go there alone, I am not so excited about it after all." She remembered her flight.

"Why not?" asked Prophet Omane. "Are you all of a sudden scared of the white man?"

"Oh don't mind her."

"Come on, why?"

"I am scared of flying again."

"Oh you didn't like it eh? You come from the country that's why." Prophet Omane said and gave a loud laugh!

"Don't tease her. It was also my first but I thought it was very nice," Kojo lied.

"Let's not think about it," Yoonko said.

Just then Araba entered the room.

"Eii, welcome lovebirds."

"Thank You. We've been married for only three weeks and Yoonko says she has missed it. How is that for a good husband?" Kojo said with a smile.

"Missed what?"

"Come on, mama a woman should know."

"Oh that's it? I will get a grandchild in nine months. Ha, ha. Very good news indeed." Araba said while she sang a love song for the married couple and danced the apatampa with a handkerchief.

"They stayed at my hotel in Accra and I knew something would happen but I didn't think it was this quick. Ha, ha, ha."

"Do you think I am a man for nothing? Look at me I am strong and powerful!" He flexed his arm to display his taut biceps. He did it again with both arms as though he were a body builder.

"You should take me to the hotel too," Araba finally said looking in the direction of Prophet Omane.

"You'll have your chance. Just exercise some patience," Omane said. "Kojo and I will also travel abroad soon."

"Ei, the way you use church money!"

"But don't you think Faith Healing Church of God will be proud if their prophets went abroad? I think so."

"Where will you go?" Araba asked.

"To the French people's country, of course. Where else?" Kojo asked.

"You mean Abidjan?" Araba asked.

"No, French Aburokyire," Prophet Omane said.

"For what?" asked Araba.

"For an international convention," Omane lied.

"And those people invited you?"

"You never heard of it eh? The name of my church and my own name are all over the world," Prophet Omane said and nodded his head aggressively.

"Ei, my future white men," Araba said with immense happiness as if being in the white man's country is the same as being in heaven.

At church service in both Kumasi and Bekwai, the self-proclaimed prophets made known their recent intentions to the congregation. Prophet Omane said that a trip to the white man's land would give much more spiritual power to serve the congregation even better.

"The Bible came here through the white man and being there with them and talking about the Holy Book will certainly enhance my knowledge and spirituality. Don't you think so?"

"It is very true," the congregation intoned and clapped vigorously.

"If it is true, then what do we need to do; all of us?"

"Contribute, of course!"

"Praise the Lord," Prophet Omane shouted at the top of his voice while clapping himself and smiling.

"Alleluia," they echoed.

"In fact, let's start a special collection today. Choir and bandsmen give us some music," the prophet said.

They sang, drummed, clapped and danced to the front where the big collection barrel was once-again conspicuously placed. The members stood row by row so that no one sat and was left behind on a pew otherwise it would be embarrassing for them due to the fact that everybody would know that they didn't contribute. Araba, waving a white handkerchief, danced to the barrel more than ten times always putting some money in to coerce others to follow. Of course, the money had been given to her by the prophet.

The same ploy was being used by Prophet Kojo at Bekwai. Yoonko, under instruction, danced many times to the collection barrel and many of the rural folk, with their little monies, put in their contribution.

"If you want to make a special and personal donation and your name mentioned, we shall gladly do so. God loves a cheerful giver," Prophet Kojo said, danced aggressively and blew his trumpet energetically at the same time. His tune, which he played over and over was,

> "I am saying thank you Jesuuus
> Thank you my Lord
> I am saying thank you Jesus
> Thank you my Lord."

He then changed the tune to

> Ahenfo hen oreba o
> Aman nyina wombo ose
> Osee ye,
> Aman nyina wombo ose.

The congregation liked this from their prophet so they danced for long minutes, contributed and as a matter of fact, had a jolly good time.

The prophets did their job well because in less than five Sundays, they had garnered more than enough cedis to pay for their trip. They went to Johnson's Forex Bureau and got some French Francs in exchange for the twenty-two million cedis they had collected.

They got their entry visas and purchased their return tickets and in two weeks they were on flight 222 of Air Afrique and Paris bound for their pleasure trip. They were going to be there for three weeks.

In France, they stayed in an excellent hotel and toured interesting attractions like the Eiffel Tower and the Arc de Triomphe. They were intrigued by the beautiful architecture, the nice cathedrals and verdant parks and gardens.

One of Prophet Omane's dreams since he was a young adult was to make love to a white girl. Many African men who go abroad fantasize about this. I don't know why. Prophet Omane was able to coax Prophet Kojo into agreeing to this fantasy. Well, it wasn't so much of a fantasy now because their hotel also ran what could be called a brothel. At dinner, the menu for food and drinks also came with a pictorial menu of very seductive prostitutes. The two prophets sampled two very beautiful prostitutes and they liked it. But Prophet Omane wanted more.

"Ei Prophet, there's AIDS!" said Prophet Kojo.

Prophet Omane decided to stop going after the prostitutes and go after some decent women. Once, the two prophets were having a quiet drink at the bar of their hotel when two nice ladies, one a golden blonde and the other, a magnificent red head entered. For some reason known to the women alone they joined Omane and Kojo little knowing that they were prophets from Ghana.

"Bon soir," Kojo said remembering his little French from secondary school. "soyez le bienvenue."

"Merci."

"Qu' est-ce que vous faites a cette heure-ci?" asked the blonde.

"Huh?" asked Prophet Omane.

"Oh sorry we don't speak that much French and we hope you understand English, do you?"

"Yes, a little," the red head said with a heavy French accent. The two prophets were encouraged.

After some apparently difficult conversation with the two ladies Prophet Kojo felt at home with the red head while Prophet Omane was very satisfied with the blonde. Prophet Omane found blonde hair very intriguing. In fact, had he not come to France he would have never set eyes on a live blonde except on color television of course. This blonde lady was very adventurous for she had already had her hand between the Prophet's thighs. The prophet had a hard-on immediately. In fact, he was so erect that he thought it was too embarrassingly visible. After a few drinks and attempts at more conversation and relaxation Prophet Omane excused himself and took off with his girl. When they got to his hotel room everything was all correct so far. Soon they were on the bed fondling each other and using more body language. The blonde's expertise at this surprised the prophet and he just couldn't wait for the coup-de-grace. He undressed first and waited for the blonde to follow. She was hesitating so the prophet thought of helping. After frantically and excitedly taking off her clothes he discovered to his greatest amazement that the blonde woman wasn't a woman. Well, she was a man with a penis and all. A transvestite! That's their name. His hair was a wig, his breasts were full and he had been wearing a very tight jock-strap.

Prophet Omane, obviously, not used to this had not recovered from his shock when the policeman asked for intercourse.

"How, What! No, no, Please get your clothes on and get out," the prophet thundered.

"Oh no, not me. You mean you've never done it with a man before. You had better do it or you won't like the consequences. I am a police officer and I can get you arrested."

"I will fight you if you attempt anything."

"Are you sure you can fight a policeman. I am well trained." The policeman proved to the prophet he knew English after all.

Prophet Omane tried to get out but the woman got in his way. No matter how hard the prophet protested he couldn't get the fake woman to stop "her" persistence. He was later forced to give in and "she" started again with her fondling. The rest can be left for the imagination. An embarrassed Prophet Omane could not believe the whole episode. He feared and debated whether to break the news to Kojo.

"Could he also have met the same fate?" asked the prophet. "What a shame and an embarrassment," he thought, much confused. When he met Kojo again he waited for him to bring up the issue about the two ladies.

"How was it with your blonde girl?'

"Everything went just right," Omane said with tears blurring his eyes.

"Really?"

Prophet Omane started to have a rapid heartbeat for he knew the tricksters had pulled the same thing on Kojo. He confided in Kojo and told him everything. To his surprise Kojo said,

"My redhead was very good."

"She was a woman?"

"Yes, why not?"

"Mine wasn't."

"What! Are you kidding?"

"No, she wasn't. She was a man!"

"How? I don't understand."

Prophet Omane sighed heavily while occasionally dabbing his eyes with a handkerchief to keep away tears. He said,

"Mine was a male with all the male accoutrements."

"But he looked every bit like a woman."

"Now I know you shouldn't trust these people. They can fool you. It is not like Ghana where such absurdity is unheard of."

"Ei, the world is very strange!"

"Please don't mention a word about this disturbing episode to anyone. It will be too embarrassing and it will certainly cast a slur on us because people will ridicule us when they hear of it."

As usual, he got Kojo to swear a solemn oath, which Kojo agreed to, for he felt sorry for his elder prophet. Case settled. There was no more dealing with girls for fear of contracting AIDS for he had heard so much about it on Kumasi radio and the connection between it and homosexuality but the episode haunted Prophet Omane and he was a confused man indeed.

The week that intervened before their departure for Ghana came rapidly for Kojo who was quite nonchalant and was enjoying himself. But the week took an eternal time to come for Prophet Omane. Finally, it was twenty-third August the day of their return. Prophet Omane was relieved and damned the French just because of the unpleasant episode.

"What if I have AIDS, Kojo?" This question was a constant worry for him and he had been losing sleep over it.

"There is no need to worry about it now; something done can never be undone as the saying goes, leave it to God."

"Oh Kojo you are not being sympathetic."

"What must I do?"

"Stop worrying you can have an AIDS test when we get home. I hope you don't have it."

After all, it was your idea that we have some white women.

In spite of such a burdened mind of Prophet Omane, the two got to Accra in one piece and proceeded to Kumasi where they were met at the airport by the Kumasi branch of the Faith Healing Church of God. They were all dressed in white and waving handkerchiefs and signing to give their prophets a rather thunderous welcome. They were indeed glad to have their prophets back.

CHAPTER 9

"Welcome my white men," Araba said.

"Thank you, thank you very much," the prophets said simultaneously.

"How was French Aburokyire? I can't wait to hear all about your exploits."

"Paris is the capital of France just like Accra is our capital and believe me the place is very beautiful."

"Can you speak French?"

"Un peu, as the French will say," Kojo said.

"Speak some French," Araba said.

"Well, France is a beautiful country."

"Yes, Kojo said it," Araba said.

"What fascinated me most was the medley of architecture. We were privileged to be on top of what the French call the Eiffel Tower. It is a very tall structure and I don't think you can imagine how it felt at all. Then there was the Arc de Triomphe."

"It was just breathtaking," Prophet Omane continued.

"What I liked most were the peoples' sophistication and the excellent cuisine."

"I even sampled some frog legs."

"Kai, Yuck, ilk! You mean some people eat frogs?" Araba was quick to ask.

"Not the whole animal. Just the muscular and fleshy hind legs!" Prophet Omane contributed again but deep down still thinking about his ordeal and the haunting possibility of AIDS. One would wonder why it was only Prophet Omane who was so concerned about contracting AIDS. Prophet Kojo might, just as well have contracted it. However, the conversation continued.

"What did you bring me from the white man's land?"

"I brought you a nice F.M. radio," Prophet Omane said.

"Is that all you brought all the way from far away French Aburokyire? Just a radio?"

"Mama don't be greedy. We each brought a video deck and camera. We also brought some very exciting video cassettes," Kojo said.

"Didn't you bring anything for your brother Father Kwesi? My own and only Father Kwesi?" The statement hit Kojo on Araba's changing attitude toward her priest son.

"Why not!? I bought him a whole Yashika camera and a fine Seiko watch," Kojo said.

For the whole day and deep into the night many stories were told of their visit. Fascinated Araba swallowed everything. It was about 1:30 am when they went to bed. Araba asked for her share of sexual pleasure but Prophet Omane declined. This was a surprise to Araba so she asked, "Why are you being so difficult tonight. I thought you missed me. What's wrong?"

"Nothing, I am not well."

Prophet Omane feared that if he had contracted AIDS from the AIDS-laden lands of the West, he could be spreading it to his friend. After much more pressure from Araba, who could not be blamed because it had been a long time since she had one, Prophet Omane was forced to use one of his condoms and seemingly satisfied Araba with condom sex, something he didn't particularly like. He usually wanted raw sex. Lucky woman. But Araba also didn't appreciate condom-sex that much. Araba was baffled.

The two prophets made a quick decision to be at Okomfo Anokye Hospital the following day.

While there, they carefully changed their identities for fear that they would be found out as many people in Kumasi had heard the prophets' names, especially Omane's.

Preliminary tests proved inconclusive. The two were referred to Korle-Bu Teaching Hospital in Accra as the AIDS equipment at Okomfo Anokye Teaching Hospital was inadequate.

Kojo went back to Bekwai. Yoonko was overjoyed to see her husband. She was very much surprised that her husband told her he had to be in Accra again.

"Why, you just came from Accra and you want to go there again," she queried.

"I have to attend to some very urgent church business as directed by Prophet Omane. In fact, I am going there with him the day after tomorrow.

All day and night, Kojo was uneasy and not quite himself because he, too, was haunted by the AIDS devil. Yoonko was much surprised that Kojo did not attempt any sex despite her persistent efforts of encouragement. She could not believe what she was seeing because Kojo was a man full of abundant sexual appetite.

The day after being in Bekwai, Kojo visited Father Kwesi at Jakobu. A felicitous Father Kwesi spread his arms around Kojo in a great display of energetic welcome.

"I am delighted you are back. How was the white man's land? You've even gained some weight I can see," Father Kwesi said.

"Thanks. France is <u>Krabehwe</u>."

"You should visit Europe someday and wow your beard, it is nice and thick and I didn't know you were growing one."

Father Kwesi used his right hand on his black beard a couple of times and said,

"Just for a change, you should grow one too after all you are a prophet. Coming back to Europe, I will work very hard to merit the Bishop's favor to allow me to travel, at least, to Rome and, of course, to the Vatican."

"Paris is very beautiful. Lovely multi-lane highways, astounding architecture and parks and exciting picture galleries. I even saw the painting of the very beautiful woman with a smile."

"They said it was painted by a great painter called Leonard Vinch."

"Oh you are talking about the Mona Lisa. It was painted by Leonardo De Vinci not Leonard Vinch as you say."

"Oh well, same thing."

"You know he was not from France why should his picture be in Paris?"

"He was Italian and he also painted the Last Supper of Jesus with His Disciples. He painted this picture on a wall in a church."

"I don't suppose it was a Catholic church," Kojo said.

"Well you guessed it, it's right. Much good has come from Catholicism after all, in fact, if Martin Luther had anticipated such a proliferation of churches and sects, especially doubtful ones and especially in Ghana, he would have tried to put things right within the Catholic church and would not have protested and become a Protestant and some of these roguish spiritual churches would not be in the country."

"Please let's not talk about this. If all your talk is directed at converting me back to Catholicism, I will tell you that I have become a die-hard prophet. I don't even know much about this Martin Luther you talk about but I know he did the right thing," Kojo said a bit angry.

"Waa look, you don't even know how your own church came to be in existence."

Kojo wanted to change the subject because he felt an extended conversation would be useless. He produced and opened his bag. Out came Father Kwesi's presents of the Yashika and the Seiko. An excited Father Kwesi was profuse in his gratitude to his brother. Kojo quickly left Yoonko and Bekwai to hurry to Kumasi to meet Prophet Omane.

They proceeded to Accra in Prophet Omane's Benz and this time with a chauffeur because the prophet was still not at peace with himself. But, at least, if he was going to die soon, he might as well enjoy the best comfort possible left. The Mercedes provided it all.

At Korle-Bu, they were kept waiting, however, Prophet Omane soon realized that he should give some kola so he brought out four five-hundred cedi bills and gave them to the nurse-assistant. The nurse quickly went inside and told the nursing-sister who came out beaming an ear-to-ear smile. Pretty soon, the smile vanished and was replaced by gloominess. There and then Prophet Omane knew she, too, had to have some kola. Another two thousand cedis changed hands. The anxiety of the prophets had built up to such an apogee that they mistook the male nurse for the actual doctor and started blurting out their concerns.

"We are two travelers from Kumasi. We went to France recently and guilty of our own indulgence we want to have an AIDS test. We have been referred here from Okomfo Anokye," Prophet Omane said with some effort and nothing could mitigate his shame.

"Sorry, I am not the doctor, just a minute."

The male nurse went in and brought the real doctor. He welcomed the couple pleasantly and some of their uptightness left them.

"Please, we are here for an AIDS test," Kojo went to the point.

"You have come to the right place," the doctor said and smiled encouragingly. He gave his routine health check then followed by the actual test. Blood samples were taken from both. Anxieties were still high but the doctor gave them a week to return for the results. Instead of going on to Kumasi and Bekwai, Prophet Omane telephoned Araba while Kojo also phoned Yoonko and said they would stay in Accra a week longer.

"What hotel should we go to?" asked Kojo.

"Novatel?" he continued.

"Novatel my foot," Prophet Omane said. "Let's go to Ambassador."

"Agreed."

At Ambassador Hotel it did not occur to them even once to pray for the Almighty's mercy. Some prophets indeed! They just lay there and brooded in anxiety. The whole week seemed like eternity but it finally came. They got back to the doctor at Korle-bu and he handed them the results in an envelope. With very trembling hands and a lot of butterflies in the stomach, Prophet Omane quickly tore it open and read it. Good Lord the tests proved negative. He read it again to make sure. He was all of a sudden beaming an ecstatic smile. It turned into a loud cackle.

"What is it?" Kojo asked.

He handed the envelope and the results to Kojo who just couldn't wait. He too, read to his astonishment and immense relief. Prophet Omane, too overjoyed to say anything, dug into his pockets and laid a flashy ten thousand cedi wad of crisp five hundred cedi notes on the table of the doctor.

"Gee, is this for me?"

"Yes, doctor," he laughed again.

"Thank you very much, I was just doing my work."

"Well, you did quite a good job," Kojo put in.

The doctor as usual gave the two a lengthy lecture on AIDS and its fatality. One would think after all this ordeal and lecture that the prophets would control their sexual appetite but how could they when their prophet hood was also tied to ensuring children for the barren.

The two prophets were very ecstatic, relieved and elated. They couldn't wait to be home. Prophet Omane relieved the chauffer and took to the driver's seat and drove flawlessly, not unmixed with terrific speed. At about 10:30 am they were home.

With immense peace of mind they relaxed in an alcoholic indulgence. Prophet Omane, inebriated, was cocky,

"No one can give me AIDS! Who, Kojo?"

"Yes no one," Kojo, also drunk, said, "Us, no one," he said the last phrase while he hit his chest hard with his right fist and spat on the ground. He used the heel of his sandal to clean the phlegm in a very stomach-revolting manner. He was obviously enjoying being drunk.

"If France, teeming with AIDS, couldn't give it to us then who would? Tweaaa," Prophet Omane said again and poured himself a fresh fill of Hennessy.

"Hey, we still have church service tonight don't you think we should take it easy on the booze," Kojo said and ironically guzzled half a glass. Prophet Omane also took half a swig and laughed boisterously, he, too, seemed to be having a jolly good time.

"Church Service can wait, Kojo."

"I must go for a grand church service reawakening. I am really going to blow the trumpet till my cheeks burst."

"Yes, Kojo, do really give it to them," Prophet Omane enjoyed the humor and laughed loudly again.

"You should come back here and burst your cheeks for my congregation. They miss you."

"O.K. but not today," Kojo said and attempted to stand up. He slumped down instantly. He supported himself on Prophet Omane's shoulder and got up, staggered into the bathroom and urinated.

He was singing so pleasurably that his urine was not directed at its right direction. After this he cleared his throat and spat into the bowl. He forgot to flush it. When he returned to where Prophet Omane was sitting, Prophet Omane was dozing already with a stertorous snore. Kojo sank into his couch, stretched out and also went to sleep.

The two prophets slept soundly for about a couple of hours until Araba woke them up. Seeing the glasses and bottles Araba knew right away what they had been doing. She cleared the table. In the meantime, the two prophets who had got up went back to sleep after Prophet Omane had wiped the slime of saliva from his mouth and part of his right cheek. His pillow was wet with saliva.

"Wake up, wake up!" she said. "Kojo won't you go back to Bekwai today?" she continued while shaking him to wake up.

"Oooh, let me sleep," said Kojo and slumped back onto the couch. Araba, with some persistence got both up and started asking them news from Accra. Prophet Omane almost told exactly why they were in Accra had it not been for the timely intervention of Kojo, who although drunk, was still sharp. Kojo told his mother of a national meeting of all prophets in the country.

"It just took longer than we expected so it has worn us out," Kojo said.

"Yes, but go quickly to Yoonko. She misses you a lot. As a matter of fact she visited me not quite three days ago."

"Is that so?"

"Yes."

Kojo got up, rubbed his eyes in the manner of a small boy and went to get ready for Bekwai, a bit of his tottery state having left him. She wanted her son to hurry back to Bekwai but she also wanted to eat a late lunch with him. Prophet Omane finally got up.

"What's for lunch?" he asked.

"Green plantains with spinach and koobi and a lot of palm oil; your favorite," she said.

In a short time, she brought the food from the kitchen and they all sat to eat interspersed with trivial conversation.

After Prophet Omane and Araba saw their younger prophet off, Kojo drove his car back. On the way, Kojo almost had a close call because as a drunken driver he was driving too fast. Surprising how the good Lord could pour His saving grace on his prophets. Yes, it is the same Almighty who shines His sun on and gives His rains to both the virtuous and the iniquitous. He reached Bekwai safe and was met by a cheerful and enthusiastic Yoonko.

During the church service that followed in the evening, the congregation were roused by their prophet's new reputation as a "been-to." Prophet Omane was receiving approbation on the same lines in Kumasi. They were certainly very glad to be back. Who wouldn't? If one had such a supportive and gullible congregation ready to do anything, surely he would be glad.

CHAPTER 10

There seemed to be something missing in the lives of Araba, Prophet Omane and Prophet Kojo. They had the inexpressive longing for something they did not now possess. Their financial position was very good yet that longing for more material gain and power was predominant.

Father Kwesi seemed to have found the fullness and fulfillment of this desire in only one person. The person who was born lowly in society, who never wrote a book or led a country. Yet after his death, countless millions have followed him and learned much from him. This man promises peace and love to those who adhere to his precepts and, who is this man? He is the Son of God, our Redeemer and Savior, Our Lord Jesus Christ. Father Kwesi had found him and brought others to him. Despite odds, he had the requisite peace of mind in his day to day activities much unlike the spiritual church trio.

Upon persistent nagging of Omane and Kojo by Araba, both agreed to let their churches build houses for them because they lived in rented premises. Araba's motives were clear. She knew the inevitability of old age was a menace which always comes all too soon, she realized how fast Christmas came around every year so she shuddered at the thought of old age.

"Why waste church money on a show of extravagance and ostentation, when you can build homes for your future security," she though. Because of this nagging question about a house, Kojo sought how best he could announce to his congregation the idea of building. He consulted with Prophet Omane about that issue. Prophet Omane always seemed to have answers to such questions and had a special way of persuading his congregation to get things done for him. He ordered Kojo to have at least two or three harvests in the year and also institute a raffle, which would be mandatory for every church member of age. That surely would be a lever for the fund raising.

"Bingo! I've got it," said Kojo.

He, meticulously, followed Prophet Omane's instructions which Omane himself was using quite successfully in Kumasi. After about a year of belt tightening of their congregations, there was enough money to start.

"Where should I build?" Kojo was in a quandary when he asked his mother about this.

"Kumasi, of course."

"But my wife comes from Bekwai; don't you think it will be appropriate to build the house there?"

"My son, have foresight! When you are no longer a prophet, you will still need to come closer to your own relations in Kumasi. So build here."

Kojo saw that what his mother was saying was right. He soon found out that plots of land in metropolitan Kumasi were very expensive and hard to come by. He sought to go to the new settlements or the outskirts of Atonsu, Nhyiaeso or Ahodwo and Kotei. After some surveying, he decided on a two-plot piece at Atonsu. His intention was to build a boys' quarters first and leave the remaining piece of land for the future when more money was coming in. Prophet Omane did not have a problem at all because just behind the church was an expanse of land quite suitable for building a two-story house.

Prophet Omane got his congregation to clear the vegetation because, as usual he maintained that working for Prophet Omane was the same as working for Jesus. He said he would always give intercessory prayers on their behalf so that they would merit God's rich and abundant favors. As incentive for hard work at the building site, the two prophets gave daily, small cash prizes for the hardest worker. Thus the construction of the new houses took off with enthusiasm with each member of the congregation trying to outdo the other just like during their group praying in church.

Pretty soon, the foundations were laid and, little by little, the two structures took shape. Building costs were soaring and their coffers were becoming almost empty. Prophet Omane and Kojo had to think of new ways to solve the problem. They remembered the use of a convention or healing crusade to make some more money. They, called for another convention, and, yes, people really attended. Surprising what the Ghanaian Christian finds in these conventions and crusades. They thronged the place for that missing spiritual something in their lives. Prophet Omane and Kojo, with ulterior motives, really knew how to hoodwink their congregations with flattery and promises. Kojo found playing the trumpet continuously not such an arduous task at all because it surely brought in the monies. The women, especially, loved being entertained and entertainment they got at the convention in exchange for their monies.

While the prophets were busy looking for money, Father Kwesi was directing a period of group withdrawal for prayer, meditation, study and instruction of the Bible. His retreat was at Buoho (not far from Kumasi) where he surely gave his retreatants a lot of spiritual nourishment. He opened them to a spiritual awareness of what lay within them. He impressed upon them about how healing and restful were the times of silence and solitude which people hardly paid attention to.

He encouraged them that, as true Catholics and Christians, they should have frequent retreats even at home where people think it's impossible.

Whereas Prophet Omane and Kojo got a lot of money from the convention, Father Kwesi gained celestial tranquility and blessing not only for himself but for the others as well. While in Kumasi, the Reverend did not fail to visit his mother.

"How is my own Osofo Moko?" Araba joked.

"Don't call me Osofo Moko, please. It's derogatory."

"Can't you be kidded just a little? I was only kidding. I am very proud of you," Araba said as she chortled. Then she asked,

"Why are you in Kumasi? On church business?"

"Something like that. I led some members of my congregation on a fasting and prayer retreat. Moreover, I came to confer with the bishop."

"I don't understand why you should fast when there is always plenty of food. Our church doesn't worry the congregation with such abstinence."

"Fasting is self-denial, which pleases God immensely. Don't you remember that even Jesus, the Son of God and God himself fasted for forty days and forty nights before the devil incarnate unsuccessfully tempted him?"

"Yes, I remember that. We just don't fast in our church. Prophet Omane always satiates himself with food and I follow my prophet for he knows best."

"We Catholics always fast during Lent from Ash Wednesday to Good Friday; don't you remember, you are an estranged Catholic? Don't tell me you've forgotten this soon."

"I haven't forgotten, my son."

"Then why all this argument?"

"I was just testing your resilience as a priest."

"Don't put your own son, a reverend, to the test."

"Have you heard about Kojo and his building?" asked Araba.

"He hinted me about it but I didn't think he had even started."

"Well, I can go to Atonsu with you to see it for yourself. Kojo cares about his mother and someday, soon, I will have a place to lay my tired head. How is that for a thoughtful and wonderful son?"

Father Kwesi felt this sharp sting of sarcasm and told his mother that in spite of the fact that she did not seem to be benefitting from him in the physical and material sense he was always accumulating enormous spiritual intercession for her.

"The day hasn't come yet, for when it comes you'll definitely know that you are spiritually covered."

Araba was smirking! Father Kwesi agreed to visit the site at Atonsu. It was August and although the sun was up it had been covered by some fast moving clouds and the shade provided was a pleasant and cool surprise from the otherwise sweltering heat.

Araba was afraid to sit behind Father Kwesi on his Kawasaki motorbike. She was so used to the coziness of Prophet Omane's Mercedes that she thought it was a debasing condescension to ride on a motorbike. She got her son to go there by taxi.

When they got there, luckily, Prophet Kojo was also around busily directing the workers in a rather tough manner about how they should go about with their work. He was more like a slave master in his ways even though the workers all came from Faith Healing Church of God, Kumasi. He was oblivious of the fact that these same members were the source of his and Prophet Omane's money and labor and that they should be treated lightly. Araba went straight to her son Kojo.

"Your brother is here with me."

"Oh Father, how do you do?"

"How do you do?" Father Kwesi held his brother in an energetic embrace and patted his back vigorously.

"Congratulations on your ability to build."

"Well, thanks."

"You've made much progress, I can see," said Father Kwesi.

"I want to meet a special deadline. I want to be here for a spell after the Christmas festivities at Bekwai and that's only about four and a half months away."

Father Kwesi took short steps round the building with Kojo following closely. The reverend nodded his head occasionally in approval of his brother's success.

"You must have a lot of money."

"Quite right," Kojo said as if all the money came from wiping his brow.

"Really, I underestimated how much you were worth. Now, I know you are really worth something."

"Thanks, I work very hard for this."

When Father Kwesi engaged some of the workers on the site in conversation, he came to the realization that they were, most of them, from Faith Healing Church of God and he knew immediately how his brother had been using his church for his own aggrandizement. He did not say anything about it (whether the exploitation of cheap labor by church members was good or bad) to his brother.

"I see you have your congregation under your arm," Father Kwesi said.

"Yes, because of my good ministering, I guess."

"As for Kojo I don't know what I will do without him. I knew I had a good and wonderful son even from his birth because I didn't even feel the usual labor pangs of his birth. It's good I didn't think about aborting him," Araba said and smiled.

"And my birth was very painful to you, eh, wasn't it?" Father Kwesi asked.

"Your birth gave me the toughest time if I remember correctly. I should have aborted you." She laughed very loud and thought it was a good joke.

"I guessed you were going to say that," Father Kwesi said also affected by his mother's laugh.

"It is true," Araba said.

When Father Kwesi looked at his watch, he knew he had overspent the visit. He told his mother that he must go but Araba delayed him some more by holding a protracted tete-a-tete with his brother. Obviously, Father Kwesi knew she didn't want to let him join the conversation. Finally, she got around and they were off to Kumasi in a taxi. She wanted her son to stay till she prepared something for him but he told her he should be going. He gave Araba some money she wasn't expecting. She didn't need it but she took it anyway and thanked him. Father Kwesi got on his bike and he was off to the cathedral.

There, he met the Bishop who expressed his appreciation for his leadership. In fact, he said his show of appreciation had been belated because he knew how far and how well his work had gone.

"Holy Father, at Jakobu, I've got some boys and girls who want to dedicate their lives to the service of God like us."

"Good for us. God bless them."

"I wanted Your Holiness, if you please, to pay us a visit to act as a catalyst to these kids who are really bent on serving the Lord."

"By all means, I will surely add a visit on my schedule. I will use part of my vacation sometime in November to pay all of you a grand visit."

"Thank you very much. Our parish will be most blessed."

"Bring more people for retreats because they are edifying."

"Yes, holy Father."

"Before I forget, I have some good news for you. I want you to carry a special message to our Most Holy Father, the Pope, sometime before Christmas so be prepared for this."

Father Kwesi genuflected in a show of gratitude to the Holy Bishop for giving him the opportunity. He always hoped and dreamt about visiting Europe and, even more, the Vatican. It was a dream come true and he looked forward to the date of his departure. When he finally left Kumasi for Jakobu, his elation was beyond words.

On the following Sunday, at church service, he announced his new luck to the congregation. They prayed for a successful trip, sang a hymn of thanks to the Almighty and clapped in appreciation for their priest's good fortune. They knew that conferring with the Pope would be an immense blessing for their well-liked Father, some of which would definitely trickle down to them when he returned from abroad.

The days sped by. Pretty soon, it was the twentieth of November. The bishop of Kumasi paid his visit to the Jakobu parish and he received a tumultuous welcome from the congregation. At the High Mass, the bishop, once again, announced to them that their priest had done exceptionally well that he was sending him on a visit to meet the pope himself. It was very welcome news for the members and to show their appreciation, they clapped for quite a long time.

Father Kwesi thanked the bishop again and ensured him and the members that the trip would be very worthwhile and beneficial to himself as well as to them on his return.

"I will bring you blessings from the Pope."

The Bishop nodded his head as if very satisfied about what he was seeing at Jakobu. After the mass, the members, in a long queue, shook hands with Father Kwesi and congratulated him.

It was early December when a few church members traveled to Accra with their priest to bid him bon voyage to Europe and to the

Vatican. He was going to spend three weeks. Though he needed just about a week to be in the Vatican, a couple of weeks had been added for a short vacation abroad.

At the Vatican, he was fascinated by awesome and solemn St. Peter's Basilica where he saw the Pope face to face for the second time. The first time was during the Holy Father's visit to Ghana a while back. The embodiment of Christian radiance was emanating from the profound, solemn and reverent Holy Father and the Supreme Leader of the Holy Catholic and Apostolic Church to the Jakobu exemplary leader. Their discourse centered on moralistic good sense, divine love for each and every creation of the most high, and finally, human interdependence as the sole basis of love. The Holy Father impressed upon Father Kwesi the importance of altruism and magnanimity.

The Bishop of Kumasi's message was relayed and given attention to during the remaining part of Father Kwesi's visit. The rest of the time was spent in sightseeing.

Included in Father Kwesi's itinerary to Europe, was, also, a stopover in France. He combined the visit to France with a prayerful pilgrimage to Lourdes. His reverence for the Blessed Virgin Mary asserted itself in a grand way. His spiritual blessing was daily amplified therefore. He just could not wait to be back in Ghana to his Jakobu parish and even to engage Prophet Kojo in a conversation on France since, now, both had been there.

While Father Kwesi was immensely enjoying his trip to Europe, time was also speeding by and the day of departure came very soon indeed.

"How time flies when one is having fun," Father Kwesi couldn't help but say to himself.

Back home in Accra, he paid a courtesy call on the Bishop of Accra before proceeding to Kumasi. After attending to the Bishop, he made time to visit Araba.

"Ei, my other white man, Welcome," she said with obvious delight. What did you bring me from the white man's land?" she continued.

"Won't you even ask me <u>amanee</u> first?! I am the traveler and I bear better and foreign news."

"O.K. O.K., Amanee."

But before that, she offered Father Kwesi some water in courteous traditional welcome. Out of courtesy and custom also, Father Kwesi accepted the glassful and drank it all even though he was not thirsty.

"Well mother, <u>aburokyire</u>, as Kojo might have related to you already when he arrived from there, is quite a place."

"Tell me more."

"Sure. First, I was in Rome the same day I left here and just the airport was enough to give an idea of what was coming. There were even computer screens at the airport itself. Computers are very intelligent and helpful machines invented by the white man."

"Why do you say they are intelligent? How can a machine think?"

"That's exactly what they do. They think."

"Wonderful! But continue."

"We traveled on magnificent roads past ancient buildings which are now spoilt by age but are kept for tourist purposes. We were finally at our destination, a place called the Vatican where the Pope, the leader of the Catholic Church in the whole world, resides. The churches were grand but the grandest of all was St. Peter's Basilica which was marked by its lavish structure and adornment."

"I am glad you went there if the place is marked by such stately grandeur and lavishness. At least, the sons of an insignificant illiterate like me have gone places."

"I haven't finished because I also went to the country where Kojo visited. I visited a sacred place, a place most reverent for Catholics because of the Blessed Virgin Mary, the mother of Jesus Christ. It was quite awe-inspiring. I don't think you can picture it just by hearing about it. You must be there yourself."

"I will be out of my element there I am so used to these rustic surroundings compared to such developed and sophisticated places you and Kojo talk about but I wouldn't mind being there. At least Prophet Omane could be talked into this."

"Kumasi is not as rustic as you think."

"Well," Araba said with a weighty sigh. "You must share experiences with your brother when you get to Jakobu."

"Sure, and that's quite an understatement."

Araba prepared Father Kwesi something to eat after which he left for Bekwai first and then to Jakobu.

Prophet Kojo was smiling when he saw his brother. Father Kwesi shook his brother's hand hard and vigorously while patting his back energetically. His presence and the whole trip brought to Kojo's mind all his exploits and most harrowing and adulterous experiences he had had in France. This time, Prophet Kojo was feeling some guilt after his brother narrated his version of the European tour. Father Kwesi gave religious gifts to his brother before partaking in the meal prepared by Yoonko.

Father Kwesi's return brought much happiness to the Jakobu parish. That Sunday, for offertory, many of the rural folk brought much produce from their farms and also some livestock to welcome their well-liked priest back. He blessed them abundantly too. He was glad to be back.

CHAPTER 11

Prophet Omane reasoned that he could disseminate his ideas through publication. He, therefore, established a bi-weekly newspaper. The newspaper made its debut with attractive reports on marriage, politics, spiritual diseases and Faith Healing Church of God as the true church of God.

Through meticulous lampooning of the other newspapers, "The Truth," as the newspaper was called, drew much attention and was a strong competitor with other newspapers as far as sales were concerned.

Prophet Omane soon discovered that the Auntie Esi question and answer column on adolescence, sex and sports was very attractive to the youth. Auntie Esi was given a two-page middle column. Auntie Esi constantly used the name of Jesus in answering the most gross of sex-related questions. The real motive of her column was obvious; to attract more and more readers and make money. In a very short time, the newspaper commanded a wide readership in Kumasi and was infiltrating the regional capitals.

On the column for politics though, the editor of "The Truth" used biting invective to discredit well-meant political decisions by the government. Everyone knew "The Truth" was treading on dangerous ground. However, it was not deterred in its quest for the truth. The political declamation did not stop until an August thirteenth publication came out. In it, it had seriously lampooned the whole junior and senior

Secondary School system and ridiculed the district assemblies. The article didn't augur well with the policies of the authorities. Therefore, Prophet Omane was summoned to the public tribunal where he was charged with political sabotage. During his cross-examination, it came to light that "The Truth" was deliberately trying to stir up political discontent among the rank and file. The prophet and his editor were jailed a month each. Prophet Omane was fined two million cedis whereas the editor was fined five hundred thousand cedis.

During their jail term, Prophet Kojo put his Sunday school teacher in charge of the Bekwai branch to fill the temporary void created by the gaoling of the church leader. For Faith Healing Church of God, the whole tribunal case was not to be viewed as a discredit for their jelly-curled prophet. As a matter of fact, it helped to send abroad the name of the church as the case made front-page headlines in the major daily newspapers.

In the aftermath of the jail sentence, "The Truth" was thoroughly investigated. To soothe the authorities' indignation a ban was slapped on it.

When the two men got out of jail, they were more than heroes in the church. Prophet Omane's prophet hood took a more vigorous turn. He looked healthy even though a jail term in this land to a person with non-mental strength will bring him to near insanity. Many women, sympathetic to the cause of Prophet Omane's prophet hood, had joined the church. His virility was great and his clandestine activities with the females were yet to be broadcast about. Araba knew all these affairs but she never alluded to them since she had had such an elevated position with her avowed prophet friend. Their bond of secrecy was unquestionable.

Before Kojo left for Bekwai again, he and his leader held private discussions with two nice looking and prominent churchwomen as far as status and position were concerned. One night, a very funny and sordid encounter occurred between the two women and the two prophets. They had prayed to the Almighty to give them a fruitful discussion on the use of church money and the need to finish the buildings under construction. They had not been at it for quite fifteen minutes when the lights suddenly went out. Black out. As if by telepathy, some pornographic movies that the two prophets had watched and enjoyed in France came to play in their minds. Both were thinking in terms of an orgy and this was a very good opportunity. Both thought of raping their women.

Prophet Omane kissed the woman closer to him softly and boldly accosted her by getting his right hand up her plump thighs. A bit shocked by her prophet's attitude, she however, did not make any noise to embarrass him as Prophet Kojo and the other woman might get to know of what was going on. Kojo wasn't the problem but the other woman. Had the first woman known that Prophet Kojo was following the same lines as his prophet she would have done something really quick. With all their protestations, the two women couldn't withstand the strength of the prophets.

The charged velvety darkness was pregnant with sexual misdemeanor. And as suddenly as the lights had gone off so it also came on again.

"Shiee!"

Continue or stop. The vileness of it all surely got the better of the two respected women and to say they were grossly embarrassed would be an understatement. Kojo stopped immediately. Perhaps his orgasmic urge had come and gone but shameless Prophet Omane, with his woman in audible sobs and protests, continued till he too got his. Ei ewiase!

The women never said a word about it to anyone because of the depth of the shame and guilt they had. They summarily withdrew from the church to the profound amazement of the congregation as they held high positions in the church. They were also big contributors to the cause of Prophet Omane's prophet hood and the long life of Faith Healing Church of God.

Prophet Omane gave a good rationalization of the women's departure and attributed it to misappropriation of funds and hence his unpleasant duty of telling them to quit the church.

Araba was still incredulous about the whole god-forsaken deal about the women's departure because they were her best friends in the church.

She sought to find out because, as she thought, the suddenness of it all was rather disturbing. First of all, she went to Prophet Omane.

"I was not satisfied with the explanation given in church about Awuraa Adjoa and Eno Aso. Were they actually misappropriating funds? I thought they were well off themselves."

"You don't believe it because it was part of the church money which they used as capital for business. I gave it to them."

'But they were always witnessing that their businesses were flourishing I didn't know they were borrowing from our church."

"It's true, Araba."

"Awuraa Adjoa and Eno Aso are a great loss to us. In fact, whenever I see them at Central Market, I will make my own enquiries."

"Forget about them. I got them out and they know I am right. I couldn't let their behavior continue to the extent of undermining and eventually ruining the church."

"They were so sincere," Araba said and sighed heavily.

Prophet Omane read into that sign and endeavored to change the subject.

"Our house is progressing just fine," he said.

Araba was pensive for a while before reacting to the new subject of conversation.

"Yes, I can see that."

"The first floor is almost done except for the electrical wiring and the plumbing," the prophet said.

"Kojo is also finishing with his boys' quarters."

"You see, if I hadn't nagged and nagged you into building you would still be renting houses."

"I am glad you encouraged us. But you know some of the church members think my two-story house is the mission house. They are mistaken," Prophet Omane said very happy that his trend of conversation had caught on with Araba.

"You should let them understand that it's your own private house in order to prevent any future bickering."

Araba surely had intelligence that surpassed that of well-educated people. Prophet Omane could clearly see her foresight and logic. He intended to legalize the possession of the house in his own name and not the church's and it was going to be done as soon as possible. Of course, Kojo astutely anticipated these possibilities and made himself the sole owner of his house at Atonsu.

By Christmas, Kojo's house was ready. He combined the Christmas festivities with the dedication of the house and church members from Bekwai and Kumasi, and, of course, Prophet Omane, Araba and Yoonko were all present. Father Kwesi was conspicuously absent. After a grand Christmas service where Prophet Omane gave a good sermon of thanks for the efforts of the congregation in terms of financial support and communal labor, they all boarded three tro-tros and got to Atonsu. There was much singing and dancing. Prophet Omane blessed the building with holy water and with a short prayer declared the house dedicated to the Almighty. At the short refreshment that followed, Kojo thanked the Kumasi branch of the Faith Healing Church of God, and, especially, those members of the Bekwai branch who gave everything to complete the building in spite of the distance. One very fat lady got up and bellowed out.

"Praise the Lord."

"Alleluia," reverberated from the congregation.

"Our thanks are in heaven because working for you prophets is the same as working for Jesus. We are happy that our prophets now have a place to lay their heads. They deserve it because we cannot measure the spiritual help they continuously and generously give us. In terms of this minimal effort of ours to build the house, Praise the Lord."

"Alleluia."

"We are dedicated to ____"

"Yes, we are dedicated to be of immense help to you anytime you call on us. Just mention what we have to do and whether it's morning, afternoon, evening or night, rain or shine, we are all ready to attend to your call," another fat lady with a child on her back cut in, Kojo took the podium again and bellowed,

"Praise the Lord"

"Alleluia"

"Alleluia," still shouted Kojo

"Amen"

"God"

"He is wonderful"

"Stick with Him"

"And you'll be free"

"Clap for Jesus," Kojo finally concluded his appellations. The members clapped enthusiastically. Everybody ate the tid-bits Kojo offered after which the members boarded the tro tros and got back to their respective homes.

Araba, Yoonko, Prophet Omane and Kojo stayed back. While they were talking about trivialities and savoring Kojo's achievement, Father Kwesi came there on his Kawasaki motorbike. He apologized for missing the dedication.

"I had you in mind all the time I was saying mass at Jakobu. You know I couldn't leave them on an august occasion like Christmas to come here, so immediately I finished with my congregation, I took my bike and came here."

"So you traveled all this distance on a motorbike just to come for this dedication?" Araba asked quite astonished and thinking that it was a bit dangerous to go even five kilometers on a motorbike.

"Yes, why not. I am an experienced rider and as I've made it several times to Kumasi, it wasn't a problem at all. Moreover, I am happy for my brother's success."

"Certainly," said Prophet Omane who had been quite evasive since Father Kwesi's arrival.

"You have an imposing building even though it's just a boys' quarters," Father Kwesi couldn't help contributing.

"Thank you." Kojo said with a grin. "Take some mineral. I know you'll say no to alcohol," he continued.

Father Kwesi took the long glassful of the Coca-Cola and downed a swig. Prophet Omane ceased drinking his Sherry for a while. He poured himself some Portello. He felt a bit self-conscious as he thought Father Kwesi had critically eyed his jelly curls.

"How is Jakobu?" Araba broke the short and awkward silence.

"Oh, everybody is doing fine."

"I am so used to Kumasi's urban Christmas. I don't suppose the rural folk celebrate it like us in Kumasi."

"How was it in our hometown? We never go there."

"People turn out in their numbers to flock churches every year." Araba, the most talkative when Father Kwesi is around, said.

"It is the same affair at Christmas in every corner of Ghana. Don't forget also that this occasion is the day for their first chicken meal of the year if they are lucky," Kojo chimed in.

"Why do you say if they are lucky?" Araba asked.

"Ei, harsh economic times. People are really poor these days," Kojo said.

"We are lucky," Araba said.

"Sure you are," Father Kwesi said.

"Will you join us for dinner?" Araba asked.

"We have mutton and goat meat. We just slaughtered the animals."

"Sure, thank you," Father Kwesi said.

"Won't you join us, Prophet Omane?" Araba asked him just to bring him into the conversation since he had been so quiet since Father Kwesi arrived.

"Yes I will, of course."

She and Yoonko went to the new kitchen where they cut the meat.

"Fufu or Jollof rice?"

"Jollof rice for me," Prophet Omane said.

"Jollof rice for me too," Father Kwesi said.

While the three men of God were waiting for dinner they engaged one another in bible discussions. Father Kwesi had facility in his explanations. No wonder because he had spent almost fourteen years at the seminary prior to his ordination. The two prophets listened attentively, marveling at the Catholic priest's expertise and knowledge of the Bible and theology.

Prophet Omane was feeling uneasy because he was limited in his understanding but kept quiet most of the time in order not to reveal his lack of knowledge of the holy book as Father Kwesi was diligently explaining away. As for Prophet Kojo, he didn't care. Prophet Omane excused himself to use the bathroom and never came back. Instead, he went to the kitchen to join Araba and Yoonko with whom he was always very comfortable.

Immediately Prophet Omane left the two, Father Kwesi asked Kojo,
"When are these two going to be legally married?
"Ask them, brother?"
"Well I thought of asking you because you are closer to them than I am."
"I don't have the slightest idea."
"But it's not right for them to be living together when they haven't said any marriage vows."
"I don't think our prophet is the type who wants to be matrimonially attached. Just like you he has a commitment to God and his congregation thinks he can do it better by remaining a bachelor prophet."
"Oh, so!"

Kojo knew what their mother was getting from Prophet Omane. She not only got companionship but also an elevated status in the church. Because of Prophet Omane, she was never in need of anything; yes anything and who would worry one's head if partnership was devoid of the onerous responsibility of legal attachment? Certainly not Araba. Kojo did not belabor the issue any longer and Father Kwesi knew he had to follow.

Pretty soon, dinner was ready. Steaming, Jollof rice came with huge chunks of deliciously spiced mutton and goat meat. For the sake of Father Kwesi, everybody decided to have soda. The five relished the savory meal so much that they all (even Father Kwesi) gorged themselves with the main meal and could not eat the dessert of fruit. After the meal, Prophet Omane lounged in the lazy chair while Father Kwesi and his brother took a walk. When they returned, Kojo wanted a ride on the motorbike. Father Kwesi happily obliged. Their ride took them to nearby Chirapatre. They turned around from there and came to Ahinsan, then to Asokwa and the sports stadium area. They made a stop at Faith Healing Church of God where Kojo showed Prophet Omane's half-finished building to his brother. Father Kwesi thought these two prophets were, material wise, very lucky. He came to the full appreciation of why many able bodied Christians, especially some Catholics, reject their Catholic faith and doctrines, and seek to become self-styled prophets and prophetesses under the pretext that Catholic doctrines were no longer sound and compatible with current ecclesiastical trends and that people (gullible and ignorant people usually can have spiritual salvation, healing, children, money, and solutions to the rest of perennial human burdensome problems through spiritual churches). The self-styled prophets and prophetesses always claim to have had a vision and to have been visited by the Holy Spirit and therefore called to minister for their churches and the Almighty. Many of them though soon lose track of this august purpose and are led to the base lucrative aspects of concrete material gain.

The two bike riders returned to Atonsu. Prophet Omane was having a nap. Father Kwesi had to go to his mother to say farewell. He asked his mother to say farewell to Prophet Omane when he got up, and headed towards Roman Hill intending to go to the cathedral.

Back at Atonsu, the two prophets decided to stay over. Yoonko wanted to come to Kumasi even though her husband still had no problem as he decided to commute between Kumasi and Bekwai. Everybody was gratified at the season's festivities. They all waited for the watch night during New Year's Eve.

CHAPTER 12

Watch night marked the eighth anniversary of Faith Healing Church of God. At the same time the Roman Catholic Church was enjoying almost two thousand years as a church and making no noise about it.

Prophet Omane and Prophet Kojo had drawn up elaborate and detailed agendas for the day. All members of Faith Healing Church of God were supposed to assemble in Kumasi, and they thronged the church.

Though it was only an eighth anniversary, the celebrations far surpassed the energy of a convention. Many other invited spiritual church leaders came to the anniversary in their luxury cars. The parking place glittered with new Mercedes Benzes, BMW's, Porches, a gold Jaguar and even a Ferrari. Prophet Omane definitely had a genius for making friends, especially big friends. His liking for them was measured solely by the completeness of their devotion to him or by their financial usefulness to him. The minute they failed him, even by so much as not attending service on Sunday or by refusal of an invitation, he would cast them off without a second thought. All his friends knew him well. Therefore, on this occasion of his church's anniversary, every friend came to please and congratulate him. Thus when they thronged in, the tuxedoed, jelly-curled prophet did not deny them his warm, smileful hello and tremendous good cheer.

He was mortally offended when Araba did not attend the anniversary but instead, went to the funeral of a very close relative. He was so grief-stricken that even Kojo's efforts (hard efforts indeed) did not mean much to him. Why? Because Kojo did not prevent his mother from not attending the anniversary.

After every invited guest was seated, Prophet Omane took to the podium, positively satisfied at the big attendance even though it was without Araba, and intoned,

"Praise the Lord"

"Alleluia," came the deafening response.

"Praise be Him."

"Alleluia"

"Alleluia," shouted Prophet Omane

"Amen"

"Clap for Jesus"

The congregation clapped louder than usual. Why all these appellations. Well Prophet Omane and Kojo couldn't believe their eyes at the multitude. In order not to bore them, the anniversary started off with free-for-all dancing as Kojo was blowing away his trumpet like mad. How the sound of the trumpet could catalyze such pandemonium was known to only Prophet Omane and Kojo. Could they be using juju to entrance this congregation? The real background behind such successful measures and attitudes by these prophets was rooted in bewitchment.

"We are very happy that you've turned out to help us celebrate this occasion. We are only eight years old but I knew we shall catch up will all the established churches because just recount our numbers in only eight years," the congregation applauded.

"We need to pray for its continuous existence, so get up everyone, and pray hard and aloud for five minutes for longer life for our dear and true church of the true God."

It was a market place now, as many people were all of a sudden possessed by the spirit of speaking in tongues.

"Jesus, Ala bra, ba, ba bra, brabaa baa bra, baa ba Jeesus! Jesus, Jeeesus, abra cadabra ba bra ba ---- Oh Jeesus Jees, Jes, Jeesus,...."

Prophet Omane was in deep glossolalia. Somebody though was deeply possessed by it too but she was speaking tongues in Hausa.

Wallahi, walla, walla wallahi, Jeesus wallahi Jeeesus, wallaaahi Jeeesus!"

Prophet Kojo who was not possessed was smirking at the show that was going on. The prayer session had gone on far too long but finally there was an immense silence brought about by a final long shout of the name of Jesus by Prophet Omane.

This silence was once more instantly punctuated by loud singing, dancing, and clapping. They came in front to the collection barrel.

"Sepe woho na bra! Asa, asa, asa, asa, mombra." Prophet Omane encouraged all of them to dance up and bring their monies. After a protracted time of money collection, Prophet Omane announced that those who could contribute or donate bigger sums of money could come up in front for general applause. More than twenty people gave up to one million cedis or more for applause.

The period of Witnessing followed the collection and it was so protracted, as every witness wanted to praise the efforts of Prophet Omane and Kojo, dutifully forgetting that every good thing came from the Almighty. It was so much that those guests who were not used to this type of witnessing were becoming bored and uneasy. Some of the people realized that some witnessing were too good to be true. Realizing this Prophet Omane rang his bell to end the testimony time.

After that, he gave his blessings, accumulated over the eight years, to the congregation. It was not just a verbal blessing. Holy water was used. He sprinkled so much of it that after the blessing, there were puddles of water on the church floor. As everyone had taken off their shoes, walking through the water was a bit uncomfortable but no one complained because only these prophets knew what was good and their interpretation of some Bible verses was impeccable. At least no one challenged them. Who would dare!? Not by just this little wet affair.

When they finally came out of the church to find their shoes, the guest with the Ferrari's shoes were stolen. They looked too nice and too expensive that one look at them will surely give anyone with long arms a very tempting thought. Other members also had their shoes stolen. They went home barefoot after they had protested vehemently to Prophet Omane. All he said was,

"God will bless you even more abundantly. Note that there is a Biblical backing for this. I am not doing this act out of my own fancy. Moses did the same thing when God confronted him. He was told to remove his sandals because he was standing on holy ground. Faith Healing Church of God's premises are holy hence the removal of the shoes." The listeners were not convinced but they accepted it. Prophet Omane was infallible!

There was refreshment for the dignitaries. Prophet Omane and Kojo recounted the history of their church again even though they had narrated it during the anniversary service. The guests finally left the church with sound impressions about Faith Healing Church of God and Prophet Omane and Kojo.

Two days after the anniversary celebration, Araba returned from the funeral. Prophet Omane would not have anything to do with her.

"You left us to have the anniversary alone."

"Well I really had to go. It was a very close relative."

"Am I not closer to you than this relative?"

"But he is of the same blood. You are just a friend."

"Just a friend? I see."

"I don't mean what I am guessing you are thinking."

"You could have left after the anniversary."

"Oh no, that would have been too late."

"What!"

"Yes, please, understand my situation."

"No."

"You had better or I will let lose all."

"Really?" Prophet Omane said, as he knew well what she was going to say.

"Why not."

"Don't you dare!"

"I, definitely, will."

Prophet Omane came on the defensive now. "O.K. everything will be alright if you promise to make amends."

"It's you rather who should make amends."

"Alright, what do you need?"

"Some more money and one sheep to pacify me."

"You've got them."

"Are we friends again?"

"I guess so."

"Thank you," Araba was simpering all over. She stuck to her guns and got what she wanted. She was happy that she had once again succeeded in blackmailing Prophet Omane.

When Araba was relishing the sumptuous meal which she had prepared with some of the mutton she forced Prophet Omane into giving her, Father Kwesi paid her a visit. The visit was brief but he had something to say to his mother while he partook in the meal, he, through some sweet words, confronted his mother.

"Mama, your living together with Prophet Omane is not right."

"What is your reason for saying this?"

"You are not married to him."

"I know, but I divide my time between here and Prophet Omane's residence. Does that bother you?!"

"Yes, very much. As a priest, I shouldn't allow this to continue. Moreover, you are getting too old for this sort of life."

"You are not the only man of God!"

"I guess so but _____"

"Well Prophet Omane is also a man of God. He wields considerable spiritual power and even has not said anything."

"Then, I think he doesn't consider it wrong. Anyway your congregation must say something about it. Haven't they?"

"Silence means consent. If they haven't said anything about it don't you think they approve of it?"

"How about yourself? Is it right or wrong? If Prophet Omane needs you that much he should seal the relationship with a marriage vow."

"I wouldn't force it on him."

"Do you want me to speak to him about it?"

"No, please."

"Then will you commit fornication with him?"

"I don't mind that."

"You see what your estrangement from Catholicism is doing to you. You, don't even care whether you are in perpetual sin."

"I just don't want to encounter a marital disaster."

"And you think it can be avoided by this cohabitation without marital commitment?"

"I do my best to keep this relationship alive," Araba said.

"I say it's all wrong, mama."

"Kwesi, I know you are a priest but I am also much older than you are. I am wiser than you and you should know that."

"Agreed."

"Let me live my own life. I know what I get from it."

Father Kwesi realized at this point that he had said and done what he could. He finished his meal in disappointment and asked to go. His mother was headstrong and couldn't be convinced. At least, he had done his part in the right direction even though he was not successful.

"I must go, mama."

"So soon?"

"Yes"

"So that's all you traveled all the way to tell me!"

"Not quite so; but the thought of it all was weighing me down mentally and psychologically. That is why I decided to steal a little time to come here. I am going back to the cathedral where I have some urgent business."

"O.K., if you are so pressed for time, then go. When do you come here again?"

"I can't tell you but be assured that I will pay you a visit sometime next month."

As soon as her son left, Araba went to Prophet Omane's residence. He was temporarily out but he soon came back.

"Hello, Araba. You are here early."

"Yes"

"What's up? Can I help you with something?"

"I just came early to tell you something important."

"Yes what?"

"I have been thinking about something lately."

"What is it? I hope it's good news."

"Our being together"

"What about it?"

"People have been watching us and they don't think it's right"

"You can get out of it if that's what you think is better for you"

"I am not thinking on those lines."

"What are you thinking about then?'

"I am thinking about marriage."

"With me?"

"Well yes. What's the surprise?"

"My dear Araba, you should count yourself lucky that we've been together this long. I want it to stay like that. Friendship. I can't be hooked by marriage."

"It will augur well for your own personality and ego."

"You think so, eh!"

"Sure."

"No, not me, marriage? No!"

"Oh prophet, come on and be reasonable. It's not such a bad idea."

"I am sure somebody has been talking to you."

"Once again, let me tell you that your proposal is not suitable for me," Prophet Omane continued.

"I thought you loved me."

"As for love, you can love someone without necessarily getting married to her. Your son, Kwesi, loves everyone but he is not married to any of them. I am just like him."

"But he is a Catholic priest. It is a vow that he shouldn't marry."

"It's the same in my church."

"Oh? Isn't Kojo married?'

"I guess so but he is different."

"But he is in the same church as you."

"Well-eh-eh…"

"You see you don't have any defense now."

"Araba, let me tell you for the last time that I don't want to be married. Enough of this heckling."

"Oh I didn't think I was heckling you; Sorry." Araba let the conversation die right there. If Prophet Omane was not going to marry her, she might as well keep the flame of their love still burning. Prophet Omane found some comfort in her being around as long as she did not rattle on about marriage. He prepared for the evening service and soon they were at the church to join the waiting and patient church members who were already singing and dancing. That evening, the service went on longer than usual as some new members were introduced and formally welcomed to the church.

CHAPTER 13

Prophet Omane truly knew why he was insistent on not marrying. Among the new members of the church, there was a very good-looking lady with the usual problem of some women. No child! Prophet Omane had taken to her right away because she was very beautiful. She was also the wife of the police superintendent.

Prophet Omane promised her that she would be pregnant. She swallowed everything hook, line and sinker and immersed herself head over heels in all the activities of the church.

To the police superintendent, the most conspicuous and detestable church program of his wife was the all night prayer sessions. The first time the wife had an all-nighter, the police superintendent was very very angry. He thundered,

"You slept somewhere eh?"

"I was in church."

"What church is this which starts service at seven thirty in the evening and closes at dawn?"

"My church does. You should take it or leave it."

"Mind your words or you'll be very sorry."

"Well, let me tell you that I have found Faith Healing Church of God and I am not ready to leave it soon."

"I am not against your going to church but you have a responsibility to me as your husband."

"I have been very reasonable over the years. What have you been able to give me?"

"Really, I don't give you anything."

"I am not talking about material things. I want a child, that's all."

"So a spiritual church can give you a child?"

"It will help me get one. In this very short time I've been at church, many former childless women have told me that their babies were the result of their faith in Prophet Omane and Faith Healing Church of God."

"Who the heck is Prophet Omane?"

"He is the prophet and the founder of the church."

"Be careful of these prophets."

"A child, I want, and Faith Healing Church of God I will go to, to get one. It will be good for both of us."

The police superintendent kept quiet. However, his current attitude showed some malevolence. He would make his own secret investigations about this prophet. The superintendent engaged the services of two C.I.D. men from the main police depot. The wife did not know these officers. He instructed them to join the church if need be. They joined.

After a very furtive, careful and thorough investigation, they reported to the superintendent that Prophet Omane was morally unscrupulous and was having sexual affairs even with very young girls.

"We found the prophet to be sexually involved with some of the members," one of the CID men told the Superintendent.

"Really!?" He said this with a missed heartbeat.

"Yes," the two CID men said simultaneously.

"Then, I suspect, perhaps, he is having an affair with my wife."

"That cannot be ruled out. The all night prayer sessions are what does it."

"Ei, women!" the superintendent said.

"What must we do about it to stop the prophet from further sexual relations with your wife," asked the taller and squint-eyed CID man.

"Never worry much, I will teach him a strong lesson."

By the way, this same Police Superintendent was selected by the Inspector General of Police and the government to lead a contingent of police officers to help to keep order before and during the independence of Namibia. He had thus undergone singular training in sharp shooting and similar preparations needed for that assignment.

Again and again the wife went for the all-nighters. The superintendent did not understand why his wife would be so irresponsible as to deny him of her marital responsibility. He was thus a very angry and jealous man indeed.

"I keep telling you again and again that you should quit the church."

"Me, quit?"

"I mean it, yes."

"You must come and pull me from the church with a tractor. Yes, with a tractor." The superintendent's anger for this cheeky remark exhibited itself in a very strong slap. The wife attempted to slap him back but he ducked to the right so that she missed him by a few centimeters. He threw a left jab. She nearly fell flat, but in an instant, she gained composure again and grabbed a beer bottle and broke it against a wall. She now had a sharp weapon. The superintendent had to muster all his police experience in order to dispossess the dangerous weapon from his wife who was now possessed by the demon of Mephistopheles. It took a long time to get the current violent aggressiveness under control but did she learn anything from this experience? It seemed not.

Meanwhile, Prophet Kojo took a week's leave of absence and was not commuting to Bekwai as before. He traveled to Accra for a couple of days to engage in important church business. When he came back, he joined Prophet Omane to conduct service. The Sunday services at Faith Healing Church of God on a fateful August twentieth day was quite extraordinary and very vividly ominous.

The morning service had been unusually long. Many people were giving fantastic testimonies and lauding their two prophets. It seemed the congregation were living in an atmosphere of Prophet Omane's personality cult.

After such a protracted service, some of the congregation did not go back home to return for the evening service. They stayed over to wait for it. Among those who waited was the Police Superintendent's wife. How some people can really serve God! If many of the citizens of Ghana could channel some of their church going energy into development projects in the country, Ghana would not be lagging behind at all in development. But people love God so much that if the whole Sunday and the rest of the weekdays were used up for church services, it doesn't spoil anything.

Back at the Superintendent's house, things were not going well. He was overloaded with anger and immense jealousy. Fixing the charcoal brazier with fire was a definite torment for him.

"Why must I have a wife and in my elevated position and stature must warm my own food? In fact, those who have children must be kings and queens," he said, and one could see he was emotionally hurt.

After eating just a bite of his supper (he just could not eat) he went inside. Surely Satan takes advantage of such emotional energy to instill in people's minds dark and terrible thoughts of violence. He loaded a pistol and headed straight to Faith Healing Church of God. It was already bustling with intense and very animated activity. The character and atmosphere of the service was singular and also sinister.

Suddenly, the Superintendent arrived in a police jeep and entered the church. All of a sudden the heated activity of the service stopped. The sudden lull changed into song again as Prophet Omane nonchalantly raised a song. When the superintendent produced his gun and gave off a warning shot, the service changed its character of immense warmth into an ice-cold silence.

"Who are you?" Prophet Omane was first to ask.

"Don't worry about my identity. I want Adwoa."

"There are many Adwoa's here.

"I want my wife."

"Wait till the end of the service. This is a church, you know."

The Superintendent directed the pistol at him as if to shoot. Prophet Omane feigned courage but Prophet Kojo, who was nearer to the superintendent, tried a very daring act. He jumped on the superintendent in an effort to dispossess him of his pistol. Two other stalwart men also advanced toward the Superintendent. "BANG!" the gun went off. Somebody fell with a heavy thud on the floor with blood oozing uncontrollably from the temple. It was Prophet Kojo. The bullet had gone between his eyes. He laid in a pool of blood.

Incensed by the unfortunate situation, every strong man in the congregation jumped on the police superintendent Prophet Omane was also incensed, however, he remained indifferent to the strong manhandling of the police officer due to the strange and current diabolical state of affairs. One evil deed attracted another like iron filings attracted to a magnet in its magnetic field.

They hit the superintendent from all directions and in an instant he lost his balance and fell heavily on the floor. The young men continued their manhandling. The place was scarlet with blood and iniquity. The superintendent collapsed and became unconscious. The oozing blood he lay in was still warming his violently battered face. Somebody who laid his hands on the fallen gun and let go of it and the officer doubled up. The Mephistophelean deed was cleanly accomplished. He was dead. There was frenzy in the church. The young men bolted. The women were now full of susurrations. They were shouting and crying. Some were running out of the church helter-skelter. Immediately, the place attracted many curious passersby.

Prophet Omane, seeing the danger which lay ahead of him immediately bolted and was at large.

Some good Samaritan helped the two fallen victims into a taxi and they were whisked off to Okomfo Anokye hospital. Prophet Kojo's and the Superintendent's situations were hopeless. Upon arrival, both were pronounced dead. An anonymous person telephoned the police and, in a flash, they were at the church premises. Upon knowledge of their superintendent's situation, they rushed to the hospital for verification.

"Dead on arrival" the doctor told them. Swiftly, they were back at the church amidst the blasting of sirens. More police help was called and the whole suburb was under police siege. Emotions were very high. The anger conspicuously written on the faces of the police officers could scare off an equally furious charging bull elephant after being wounded. Immediately, the church was ablaze. Prophet Omane's home was also ablaze. The conflagration was heightened by the electrically charged solicitude of the whole place. All the citizens were afraid and indoors with their doors heavily bolted.

A search party was swiftly dispatched to bring Prophet Omane and other members of the church including the Superintendent's wife to book.

The innate cowardice of the citizens needed no reference. It seemed as if there was a dusk-to-dawn curfew on the whole place as no one dared to come out. Gunshots were fired intermittently. Some were still warning shots. Others were for imagination to discern. Such was the tense silence of the morning, which followed the frenzied state of affairs the night before.

In the morning's newspaper, the front page caption was, 'Murder In a Church.' The sub-caption was 'Church Leader and Others Wanted Dead or Alive.' Prophet Omane was still at large. Araba, who was with him, had shrewdly begged him to drop her off any place but with him. She got her wishes fulfilled with her heart still pounding in a jet race. Somehow, she got to Father Kwesi's place at Jakobu. He welcomed her.

"Why are you so afraid?" he asked.

"Haven't you heard it, my son!?"

"About the deaths in Prophet Omane's church?"

"Yes, son."

"Certainly, I have. It's on the radio and in the newspapers. I was on my way to Kumasi."

"Well…" she sighed heavily. "We are in big trouble, all of our church members."

"Cool down, mama something can be done."

Father Kwesi allayed her fears with soothing words and very comforting intercessory prayers. Araba was crying out of fear.

But back to Prophet Omane. Where was he when all the place was being combed from house to house? He had changed transportation and was traveling incognito and heading towards Dormaa Ahenkro. His whereabouts were a mystery but the police were equally committed to clear up the mystery. By radio communication the police barriers were mounted all over the country.

With intuitive astuteness gaining the upper hand, Prophet Omane diverted his course. His new destination was Bawku and on to the border post at Kulunguugu. He had been lucky enough to defy all police recognition until at his final destination of the Upper East border post where his luck ran out. A suspicious customs officer recognized the prophet and alerted the Bawku police. Immediately, Prophet Omane was surrounded by heavily armed custom's officers. He was detained in the Kulunguugu customs cells overnight under very heavy armed guard.

The next day, he was taken to Bolga and then to Tamale all under very heavy armed guard. From Tamale, he was flown to Kumasi on a military aircraft.

In the interim, however, Prophet Omane had received his share of police revolutionary discipline despite the fact that he was a man of God.

At Kumasi, he was caged as a criminal and paraded through the principal streets where his shame and embarrassment were profound until his death, which he could discern was so near.

The death of the Superintendent proved to be a big loss not only for the Kumasi but also for the country and Africa as a whole.

After a careful tribunal case, Prophet Omane was to face the firing squad, which he accepted as an escape into martyrdom. At least, that was what he thought. On September twentieth, he was executed.

Araba was a shattered woman after having lost two very close people. Life did not, naturally, mean the end of the world. She received condolences and consolation from many people especially from Father Kwesi. He still extended his invitation to his mother to go back to Catholicism. She accepted. A contented Father Kwesi asked her to come to the Amakom parish where he was going to conduct mass at the special invitation of the parish priest of Amakom.

At the time of the sermon, Father Kwesi seized the opportunity to preach with power and fervid eloquence the homecoming of Araba as symbolic of a future return to the Catholic Church of many dissidents. He elaborated on ecumenism and said that one day soon (he hoped), the only "Una Sancta Catholica et Apostolica Ecclesia" will lead the unified Christian church with the Holy Father, the pope, as its head.

He went further and said that Jesus Christ who kept the church before the advent of Martin Luther still keeps it today and will continue to keep it till kingdom come. He lambasted vehemently, the demon-filled Catholic priests who sought to destroy the church by grand double sins of child molestation and homosexuality which are decried by the Bible.

With the benefit of hindsight, Araba, clearly, realized that she had done a big disservice to Catholicism when she quit and drew people away from it. Now, though, she was happy that her exile into spiritual church prodigality had come to an end despite the fact that it landed on a very sad note of loss of human life. She was very eager to embrace Catholicism again. It was reflected in the fact that she had gone to confession after being really sorry for all her sins. She partook in Holy Communion, a first in a very long time. Praise the Lord.

Printed in the United States
By Bookmasters